The Boulevard of Life

The Boulevard of Life

Jason Felix DeCesare

To contact author:

The Boulevard of life / Facebook

ISBN-13: 9780692605264
ISBN-10: 0692605266
Library of Congress Control Number: 2015960693
Coffee House Publishing, Providence, RI

Believe nothing. No matter where you read it, who said it,
even if I have said it, unless it agrees with your own reason
and your own common sense.

~Buddha

Dedicated to Kaldi, without you, this task would have been insurmountable.

Table of Contents

CHAPTER 1

⚜

At the Beach in Mexico

THE TEMPERATURE WAS eighty-eight degrees and the cloud-less sky allowed for the sunshine to radiate unobstructed. I sat with my back gently resting against a lone palm tree, the laws of gravity and the weight of my being created a comfortable indentation in the surprisingly cool white sand being protected by the feather shaped leaves above. I sipped a concoction of local tequila with an assortment of far too many fruit juices to name, all of which were pooled inside a freshly hollowed out coconut. This medicinal elixir was crafted by a local on the beach for us gringos attempting to escape our melancholy existence for just a few days. On my head I donned a hat made of palm fronds from yet another local merchant who demanded twenty dollars for his creation. I had offered ten.

"Ay Dios mio. Twenty dolla señor."

"O.K., fifteen."

"No Señor, veinte dolares, cheapa den K Mart Señor," the merchant had claimed, with his broken English dialect that was much better than my broken Spanish dialect.

Obviously the local with his brown, suntanned skin had observed the same sunburn on my pasty, Elmer's glue skin that I had been feeling for the last hour. Having lost the barter face off, I reluctantly handed over a twenty-dollar bill for a ten-cent hat.

Was the seller even aware that he had just defeated the previously unbeaten king of bartering? He had no idea that the man who had just lost the face off was unconquered in the art of haggling insignificant pieces of junk, such as shot glasses and corse, multi-colored blankets whose buyers' friends and family back home would never use unless they needed to sand a deck. I'd once even haggled my way to acquiring a ridiculous, three-foot sombrero that had accompanied me through Customs like an uncooperative six- year-old child, only to be discarded a few months later by my wife.

Approximately twenty feet in front, my sunscreen-covered daughters were playing in the surf. One was performing her latest gymnastics routine while the other was lost in an unrealistic quest of attempting to trap hermit crabs in the formless ocean water with a mere six-inch, constantly eroding wall made from beach sand. A few feet behind the children stood my beautiful wife. She was facing the water, thus giving me an unimpeded view of her backside. Even after two kids, her figure still looked perfect to me. I considered myself lucky that I still found my partner desirable, having never fallen into the pitfalls of marriage like so many of my friends and coworkers. Most complained about having sex with their wives. "It's like a friggin' job" one always said, another, that he would rather pleasure himself over the bathroom sink than be with a ready and willing partner. Not me. I still lusted after my wife as much today as I had ten years ago when I'd first laid eyes on her at the local coffee shop, still remembering exactly what she purchased that day. A cafe mocha with an extra shot of espresso. I hate café mocha; I should have known.

"Hemingway? *James Hemingway.*"

CHAPTER 2

———— ⚜ ————

Please do not judge me

My daydream quickly turned into a nightmare as I refocused my eyes and recoiled back to reality. I looked around to hear the family court officer call out again:

"Hemingway, James Hemingway?"

I took a deep breath, and somehow hoisted myself up from the long wooden bench that must have been designed to warn people just how uncomfortable this experience would be. The unforgiving plank awoke memories of two separate but equally depressing aspects of my youth, the seat outside the principle's office that I'd been called to on more than one occasion and, the church pew I had fought to sit still in every Sunday morning of my childhood. Why couldn't they provide a few recliners and a wet bar in family court? Maybe then it would be less contentious than sitting on a bed of nails.

I stood and straightened out my tie, making sure that it was perfectly high and tight around my neck, similar to a noose and double checked that my phone was on vibrate, I walked towards the officer that was loudly calling my name.

"I'm Hemingway sir."

"Any relation to the author?" asked the officer.

"No sir," I answered.

"Too bad, I love <u>Old man and the Sea</u>; that Santiago was one determined bastard," the officer said, only vaguely aware that I wasn't in the mood for idle chitchat.

"Court room Five D sir, that's where your case is being held. Good luck," the officer said with a sympathetic look on his face, much like a guard would give a condemned man that he befriended on his way to the gallows.

"Thank you officer," I replied. Though it was the worst day of my life, I still found in necessary to be polite and respectful.

As I walked down the hallway lined with misery, contempt and incompetent attorneys, I savored one last sip of the bitter, lukewarm coffee that I'd purchased from a blind man working in the cafeteria, and reluctantly threw it in the bin. I felt guilty discarding the Styrofoam cup, but there was no place to recycle in the courthouse. Apparently they cared about the environment as much as they did a father wanting to spend time with his children. "Courtroom Five D" I whispered out loud to remind myself where I had to go. I wondered what the "D" stood for. Death? Demise? Destruction? Devil? Disgust? I would soon come to the conclusion that it stood for Disloyal.

There she stood, the disloyal one, the one who had delivered a deathblow to my heart. She had been the extinguisher of my soul fire and I could still smell the stench of its spray, like she had filled it with urine. She was still as beautiful as ever, in her short black mini skirt, business suit top, and high heels, perhaps even more so now that I knew I would never be able to caress her aforementioned perfect ass. Even now, after she had shattered me in more ways than one, I still loved her. My shrink told me that love is based on completely irrational thought processes. Obviously she was right I mused. How else could the persistence of such feelings for the person that had ruined me be explained - other than complete insanity? I knew that the most difficult person not to lie to was myself and I couldn't lie, especially to myself. For some perverted reason I was still in love with her. As if to rub cayenne peppers into the gaping wound that once housed my beating heart, she looked at me as if she had *never* loved me. Though her beauty was a mile wide, it was only an inch deep.

As I cast my memory back and dissected the marriage, I realized it was indeed likely that my wife had never truly loved me. But as love so often does, it blinded me, and I wasn't able to see that she was never genuine with her care of my soul. All those "I love you's," she had uttered with the open-eyed kisses that were void of passion . . . there were so many signs. There were so many signs that were missed, perhaps intentionally missed, but regardless, still missed. I sighed, calling myself a fool. Deep down inside I knew my love for her was wrong; one would have to be insane to still love such a person. I wasn't a very religious man, in fact I hadn't been to church since my mother stopped making me attend after my confirmation in high school, but as with all tragedies, I had begun to pray. I prayed so fervently that there was no way God could not have heard me. I prayed repeatedly that the next day – that day – would be the day I stopped loving her, and that the stomach aches and sleepless nights would soon end, but they hadn't. I often joked to myself that perhaps God was busy with the Middle East and didn't have time for my pettiness. I talked to friends, read self-help books, even went back to a shrink, but still I couldn't heal. I wanted to stop loving her, but it wasn't up to me. Time, and only time heals, and apparently not enough had passed since she had decided to walk out on our marriage. I had to eat, but I didn't; I had to sleep, but I couldn't. I had to move on, I just didn't know how.

I could survive the day by putting on a false smile and engaging in meaningless pleasantries, but as night fell it was a completely different story. The night had power over me. The black magic of the darkness weakened my soul and the sadness would intensify. A drink . . . or even eight, couldn't erase such effects. I'd attempted that medicine on more than one occasion. I was defenseless to the negative thoughts that brought me to an ugly place most nights. My shrink had told me that I controlled my thoughts and that my thoughts did not control me. Maybe so, but knowing that information did nothing to stop the demons from coming over me every night.

"God damn it," I said to myself, as I was digesting her beauty and noticing her newly purchased breasts. I looked ahead to see a female judge, complete with a short-cropped haircut and thick brimmed glasses perched on the end of her nose. She rose up from the floor like a gargoyle who sits on the corner of a skyscraper. Her facial expression was contemptuous; she looked as pleasant as a root canal. I could just feel the negative energy that was emanating around me. I pondered what she might be wearing under that black robe. Was it a mint green pant suit with a pair of nude colored pantyhose complete with full-bottomed briefs pulled up over her belly button, leaving a red mark due to an extra ten pounds of unwanted fat around her waist? Or was she hatched, thus not requiring a belly button? Or perhaps she donned a one piece leather, sadomasochist zippered outfit, had pierced nipples and wore eight inch patent leather high heeled boots that came just below her knees. I envisioned her right hand discreetly gripping a leech that was attached to an out of shape man with a candy apple ball gag in his mouth, only to be removed during recess so he could drink from the dog bowl that was under her desk.

After the complete lack of empathy she displayed for me, I was positive that it was the latter of the two. Judge Grim gave me the standard proverbial slap in the face of every other weekend visits and crippled me financially. Apparently the judge didn't care as much as I did, that my wife had been having an affair for the past year and a half of our marriage.

When her Honor decided to remove her fist from my colon, I walked out of courtroom Five D, bowlegged, but still under my own volition. I walked past the trash bin into which I had tossed out my burnt coffee twenty minutes prior. Twenty minutes, that's all it took for a politically connected person to render her politically connected decision to display her politically connected superiority.

I most likely would have faired far better if I'd had an attorney, but I had walked in a defeated man. I thought that any person with a heart and common sense would see what had occurred and who had been responsible for the demise. I was now very personally aware that the court system was designed not for fairness and equality, but for attorneys to make a fortune.

For some reason the court officer that I spoke to twenty minutes prior to my defeat approached me in an attempt to lift my spirits. Maybe he observed the same pain on my face that I felt in my heart.

"Things will get better pal."

"They can't get worse," I replied.

"God has a plan for all of us" the officer told me.

"Really," I replied, a bit annoyed. "If your god's plan included my wife sleeping with another man, or men, not quite sure of the number anymore . . . but like carpenter ants and cockroaches, when there's one, there are usually many . . . if your god's plan was for me to lose everything - my children, my house, my money, and now requires me to move into some rattrap above a Chinese restaurant, where I'll be able to smell every time some asshole orders the Kung Pow chicken - then I don't want that god in my life. My god, whomever and where ever he or she is, is love, peace, tranquility, three things that don't exactly exist in my life right now."

"You said "right now." Don't give up on HIM just yet my friend. God has a plan; this was meant to be," the officer said as he walked away to separate two people beginning to raise their voices at one other.

As I was exiting the courthouse through the glass doors, I observed all the poor souls removing their belts and shoes, along with emptying their pockets of cell phones and change prior to walking through the metal detectors. One guy actually had a smile on his face. Either it's his first time in this place, or he has gas, I thought to myself. Hopefully for the officer's sake, the man is just ignorant to the beating he is about to receive.

CHAPTER 3

———— ⚜ ————

Changing Channels

ONCE OUTSIDE, I noticed people going about their day, seemingly living great lives, much better than mine. I watched one well-heeled couple waiting at the traffic light, laughing and smiling as they sat on imported leather seats surrounded by exotic woods that come standard in a luxury car. As I continued down the sidewalk, I came across a police officer directing traffic around a large hole in the street caused by a water leak. The police officer was not the typical one portrayed by Hollywood with thirty pounds of unwanted fat hanging over his gun belt and a mustache that would rival a nineteen seventies porn star. No, this officer appeared to be in great shape and spirits, smiling and making small talk to passers by. Even though it appeared that he hadn't eaten a doughnut in years, he was holding a coffee cup from the doughnut shop a block away. "Definitely skim milk in that cup," I said out loud to no one in particular.

I cleared the cement dust from my eyes as I continued past the construction site and noticed a homeless man sitting Indian style with his back up against the wall, both literally and figuratively. The man had a handwritten sign resting in his lap. In sloppy letters, it read "Will kill pop star for food." A+ for creativity I thought, as I put a long forgotten smile on my face. I reached into my pocket and placed more money than I should have in the used coffee cup that doubled as a tip jar.

"God bless you sir, thank you," said the homeless man.
"Don't thank me, I did it for Karma," I replied still smiling. "You brought a smile to my face - haven't had one in a while, and I need all the positive energy I can get."

"I'll say a prayer for you tonight," encouraged the man who was living on the street.

"Say two, I need 'em."
    After my exchange with the homeless man, I rounded the city block and walked into a small breakfast and lunch diner. It was a place where police officers, union workers, lawyers and judges alike grabbed a quick, consistent meal. I placed my order to go, and patiently waited in line behind the people that had ordered before me. I would normally have sat at the counter but I wasn't in the mood to exchange nonsensical pleasantries with some random waitress at this particular moment. I wasn't interested in her child's' latest accomplishment, how big her grandson was getting, or what car troubles she was having. Everyone has troubles and everyone is proud of their children, I get it. I just didn't want to hear it today. While waiting for my order, I turned around and there she was, my wife, actually, for the first time, my ex-wife. She was

sitting, holding hands across the table with her new boy-friend, well, new to me, not to her. So I was finally seeing the man that had ruined the marriage. No, wait, I realized more accurately, he didn't ruin it, she did. He was just a stranger that didn't require an obligation of loyalty.

They were too busy laughing and talking to notice me, but I noticed them and the damage was done. My heart grew heavy and a knot instantly developed in my stomach. Just as I felt the urge to vomit, the woman behind the counter instructed me to have a wonderful day and handed me the sandwich. I exited and still feeling sick to my stomach, in no mood to eat my Italian grinder with no onions and extra mortadella, handed it to the future pop star assassin as I walked by.

"Make sure you say that prayer for me," I said as I handed the grateful man my sandwich.

"I promise I will. We all walk though the valley of the shadow of death once in a while," the homeless man called out as I continued to walk down the street.

"I'm there now," I answered from twenty feet away.
"Well, keep walking."
I somehow managed to place one foot in front of the other, with my head down, hands in my pockets, kicking the imaginary can down the street all the way to my Asian import, which had an odometer that read one hundred sixty eight thousand

two hundred and sixty three. As I placed the key in the lock and manually opened the driver's side door I began to ponder once again. I came to the realization that maybe, just maybe, the wealthy couple I observed earlier wasn't as content as they appeared. Why did I assume they were happy because they were well dressed and driving an expensive car? Maybe that man's loving, faithful wife was at home with his young children while he was out screwing the office whore who, besides performing one hell of a blow job, was completely unqualified for any position she has ever held, except on her knees. Or maybe he was an ornery, impotent, bastard who was in debt up to his hairline that I could tell had been resuscitated by a doctor and some hair plugs. Maybe she was an empty soul, unable or unwilling to love anyone beside herself unless he bought her two thousand dollar pocket books and red bottomed pumps. Yes, she was probably the kind of woman who would leave him and his endless supply of Viagra the minute he couldn't afford her lifestyle, a lifestyle she has never earned, just come to expect.

Maybe that seemingly pleasant police officer wasn't in as good spirits as I had thought; perhaps the things that he'd to do in the scope of his duties troubled him. Even though he'd been cleared by a grand jury for using deadly force didn't mean that his soul was at peace. Did he have to pull the trigger as quickly as he had? Possibly, if he had yelled, "drop the knife" one more time, the suspect would have listened, even though the previous five times he hadn't. Maybe he could have continued to back up another ten feet, even though the previous ten feet didn't matter. The Grand Jury had said that five times and twenty feet of sidestepping was enough, but his conscience didn't. Or maybe it was the memory of that small black child he had carried out of the burning building; if only he had gone into her bedroom before checking the other two first, she could have survived. Most likely it wouldn't have made a difference, but an unsettled soul is very powerful in the dark silence of the night.

I turned the ignition key and, just like the previous twelve years, the car started right up. "This is about the only reliable thing I have in my life", I said as I encouragingly slapped the steering wheel. It always bothered me that I had to buy an import from Asia. I loved my country and wanted to support working class America, but American cars weren't known for their reliability after sixty thousand miles. As the car's ignition turned over, the music shocked my eardrums as James Taylor sang *Mexico* from the radio, at a much higher volume than I recalled leaving it. Was there a volume fairy that turned the radio up when you were gone? I wondered. That was the last song that I needed to hear now. It was *our* song because we traveled to Mexico every year to celebrate our anniversary. Was it a sign? A coincidence? Did she still love me? Did this mean we were going to get back together? Or was it just a completely random event, in an even more completely random world? After all, we are just floating on a speck of dust, traveling through an infinite amount of nothingness at speeds of sixty six thousand miles per hour. I wasn't sure where I stood on religion. The only truth I was sure of was that religious disputes had caused more deaths than disease and famine combined. Nonetheless, I still felt connected to a higher power and said a prayer every so often, mostly on airplane take offs and at funerals. I never understood how, in a world of constant change, religion stayed the same. I wasn't sure if I had lost religion, or if religion had lost me. All I knew was that I believed in something, perhaps a being or some overarching energy. Life was too perfect to be a mistake. I believed that coincidences were God's way of letting us know that He was present. Everyone that I knew had experienced at least a few bizarre happenings that were too foolproof to be accidental and purposeless. Whatever that belief was, that was my religion - my god. But, regardless of my beliefs, I was not strong enough to listen to that song right now and changed the channel as fast as I could. I wasn't strong enough to drive in silence, so I changed the channel to talk radio and listened to blowhards and their listeners complain in unison about the latest news story.

Knowing how diabolic my ex was, I wondered if she had placed a request with the DJ, or would the horns on the top of her head interfere with her cell phone reception, or would her forked tongue make it difficult for the DJ to hear her? One day I would be over her and she would be nothing more than a distant memory, but today was not that day. I would like nothing more for her to get run over by a bus leaving that diner. I could never harm her myself, but neither could I lie. I wanted nothing more than for her demise. When I would hear of a fatal car accident, I would get my hopes up until I heard the name of the poor bastard that actually did perish. "God, how awful am I?" I would always say when I caught myself thinking that way. I often wondered, did the person that I just heard about dying in that car accident have an ex? Had the deceased' ex wished for the same tragic ending to his ex's life as I did for hers? If so, how did they feel when their dark perverted wish actually came true? Did that person wish the same tragic ending to his own life as I did to mine?

My head was heavy. I barely had the strength to hold it level and focus on the simple task of driving home, well, not home anymore. Home is where the heart is, and hers was gone and mine was broken. What remained was nothing more than a sixteen hundred foot structure made out of 3/8th foot dry wall, two by fours and a thin layer of stucco. As I opened the door I realized that the home was void of meaning. I looked around and stopped to stare at the newly installed, un-christened, granite countertops. I had put them in right before she filed divorce papers and had me thrown out. Judge Grim had given me two weeks to collect my belongs; after that, my ex could dispose of them. That was thirteen days, twenty-three hours and forty-five minutes longer than I needed. I conducted a final walk through of each room, stopped at the doorway of the room my daughters shared, and looked at their framed drawings hanging on the wall along with their neatly made bunk beds. I stood on the threshold and said a simple prayer to whomever. "Please take care of them, when I can't. Thank you." Why did I find it necessary to thank God at the end of a prayer? Was God not going to provide my children with protection if I wasn't polite? I walked down the hall into the living room where I had put the box filled with my coffee maker, favorite coffee mug, a record player and a few of my favorite albums along with some clothes - none that she had bought me, though she had rarely made it a habit to buy me anything. She had once bought me cologne but only because *she* liked how it smelled. As I opened the door to leave I stopped, walked over to the mantle and took two pictures, one of my daughters on Christmas morning, the other, a picture I had taken with a disposable camera on the best day of my life, and even though it reminded me of pain, it also reminded me of happiness and love. It was of a lone palm tree, left of center, with the vast ocean in the background. That palm tree had withstood storms alone, and yet it remained strong, determined to survive. The palm tree didn't need another by its side to provide strength to withstand another storm. It was, in fact, more beautiful by itself; that lone palm tree could persevere on it's own, and so could I. That picture provided me strength, an attribute that I would surely need in the coming months.

I opened the door to leave for the last time, the same door where I'd been the recipient of countless hugs and kisses, the same door that I'd walked through every Friday evening like clockwork holding freshly cut sunflowers for my faithful, loving wife. Just as I was standing on the threshold of that door, I felt an urge to urinate. I put down my box and walked into the master bath that was connected to my former bedroom, lifted the seat and relieved myself. This will be the last time I will ever stand and urinate here, I thought to myself. Her new boyfriend will be the one standing in this exact spot, holding his hopefully below average sized penis in his hand. I finished and zipped up my pants, leaned down with my left hand to flush the toilet, but hesitated, and against my better judgment, decided to leave yellow tinted water there for the next guy. As I walked out of the bathroom, I looked back at the still raised toilet seat and started to laugh at how immature I was. "Fuck it." Anything besides dunking her toothbrush or the new one that accompanied hers in the toilet was a victory for both parties. I had always prided myself on taking the high road throughout my divorce. "There was great solace in being the good guy," I always said, but still, I didn't flush.

I was hypnotized on the drive from my old house, not from the perforated lines separating the lanes of travel; this time it was based solely on the fact that the life I once knew and loved had ceased to exist. It felt as though I was driving in my own funeral procession, and since my life had died, I guess I was. How could I have been such a fool? God, I'm an idiot, I thought. All those late night text messages along with the perfectly timed cell phone battery depletion on work trips, her coworker that she had to comfort after dinner - a dinner most likely prepared by me. But at the very least I should have picked up on the changing underwear pattern, that and her ever-growing supply of excuses for not wanting to be intimate.

"Stevie Wonder had nothing on me," I said to myself.

By the time I became lucid again, I was miles from my old house, having no recollection on how I had traveled to my current location. I knew that I had to refocus, so decided to pull over and purchase a newspaper along with a cup of 99-cent coffee from a convenience store. I fancied myself as a coffee connoisseur but this select your own size coffee for .99 cents did not pass muster. Like everything else in my life right now, I expected the coffee to suck. I sat in my car looking through the classified ads to find a place to live, well not live, so much as to exist. I found a few apartments that seemed to be within my budget, but none were in an area in which I wanted to exist. I pulled back onto the road heading nowhere in particular, like a hiker without a compass or a boat with a broken rudder, until I drove past a motel. The motel was nothing more than a cluster of approximately twenty dilapidated; freestanding cottages that were in desperate need of paint and a lawn that needed trimming. Each cabin was no bigger than the standard sized dorm room, so close to each other that one could most likely hear the annoying rubbing sound of skin whenever the neighbor decided to masturbate. These were the same cottages that my wife and I had driven past countless times on the way home from the beach, each time wondering the reason why people would ever stay there. The cabins were always empty except for the third one from the end on the left. We could always tell by the different cars parked in front of that unit. I would joke that the cottage was the only one with indoor plumbing and a roof that didn't require a half dozen buckets underneath every time it rained. Perhaps an illicit couple engaged in a cheap rendezvous for some extracurricular activities, or maybe an outlaw from deadwood Arizona who's on the run after committing a series of bank robberies. Or could it be some poor sap who'd researched it online and was bamboozled into paying to stay there due to a misleading website, a website I'd researched for entertainment one evening with my wife over a few glasses of wine and no sex. The pictures on the site must have been taken twenty years ago when the pool was actually filled with chlorinated water and the cottages were freshly painted. I'd determined that the photos were old from the mustachioed man, holding a cigarette, standing by the pool in a pair of tight swim trunks that barely came past his crotch, that and his hairy chest were a dead give away that the photo was taken from a time since past.

I had nine thousand dollars to my name, half of my IRA worth eighteen thousand. Although I'd worked hard to earn and save every penny, Judge Grim in her leather spiked heels had deemed my ex deserving of half. I needed to prolong my money, stretch it further than I used to pull Stretch Armstrong's limbs as a child, so I decided to make a U-turn and head back to the motel. As I pulled up, I noticed that there wasn't a ninety-degree angle to be seen. One cottage was leaning at least eight inches to the left completely encased in overgrown ivy; presumably the only adhesive holding it together. The in ground pool that was surrounded by a rusted fence hadn't been filled since Carter was in office. The grass was overgrown and overwhelmed by weeds. All the cottages were in desperate need of paint. A gallon of paint is twenty dollars for Christ's sake, I thought. The only redeemable qualities that they all shared were cathedral roofs and a small farmers porch.

As I exited my car, I stepped onto an uneven dirt drive that was in need of a few more truckloads of crushed stone to make level. An older man quickly exited the cabin at the very end of the unit. As I approached, I couldn't help but notice that the man was wearing a cowboy hat, an article of clothing rarely seen in this region, except at country western concerts, worn by teenage girls with Daisy Duke shorts. He was a thin man who appeared to be in his late seventies, but I quickly observed that he was still in great shape, not for his age, but just in general. The man wore a light blue and white checkered long sleeve shirt with the sleeves rolled up just under his elbows, displaying an illegible tattoo on his forearm that was obviously much older than I was. But unlike a multi millionaire politician trying to connect with factory workers while stumping on the campaign, he didn't remove a Rolex and replace it with a Seiko moments before the introduction; this man was genuine.

"Can I help you, kid?"
"I'm just wondering what the deal is here?"
"The deal? What are you, a reporter or something?"
"Oh, no sir, I just, I'm kinda lost right now in more ways than one, and I didn't know how someone goes about renting one of these?"

"They talk to me, that's how."

"Ok, could you show me one please?"

"Sure thing", and without hesitation, the old man started to walk towards the cabin that seemed to be the only one ever occupied. "I am such a loser," I told myself, not for the first time, and certainly not the last. Unfortunately such a statement had become a reoccurring theme in my internal dialogue.

"What's your name, son?"

"Uh... Hemingway sir, James Hemingway," as I stuck out my right hand.

"Are you related to the guy who wrote those books?"

"I wouldn't be here if I was sir." I always referred to older people as sir or ma'am, not as a sign of submission but rather as one of respect.

"Good, because I don't need any hot shots here. I met him once down in the Keys on a fishing trip though, seemed like a nice enough fellow, holy shit could he drink."

The man extended his hand as well, and returned a firm shake.

"Everyone around here calls me Tex." The everyone to which he was referring escaped me at the moment, but I nonetheless obliged.

"Nice to meet you sir, I mean Tex."

We walked onto the uneven porch of cabin number three, it was covered in a green outdoor carpet that reminded me of the times I had played miniature golf as a child. The only things missing were a windmill and the open mouth of a demented clown. What were not missing on the front porch were an old wooden chair and a bright red metal cooler. Tex opened the wooden screen door - that was missing the screen.

"I have to replace that," he said, Tex allowed the doorframe missing a screen to rest against his hip while he unlocked a solid wooden storm door that squeaked so perfectly that it could have doubled as an entrance to a haunted house. After the haunting stopped, I entered the cabin and noticed dark paneling covering the walls along with an old, musty smell. It must have been from the wall-to-wall dark green carpet or the dark green bedding on the full sized bed in the middle of the single room. To the right was one long mint green Formica counter top separated in the middle by a sink and a two-burner cook top. The only piece of furniture that separated the kitchen space from the bed was an old, dark brown, round wooden table with the matching chair from the porch that was kitty cornered next to the bed. The table doubled as a nightstand and a dining table. I had not an inkling of who Chico was, but he was there in nineteen eighty-three, or so said the three inch letters carved deeply into the top. I wondered how many cheap bottles of Whiskey and economy beers had been consumed at Chico's table to dull the pain of life's trials and tribulations.

"I'm sure I'll be adding to that number, I said to myself. "Where's the fridge?"

"That's the cooler on the porch; the old one shit the bed and I haven't gotten around to replacing it yet."

I began to notice a pattern. As I exited, Tex inquired as to what my thoughts were.

"What are you thinking?"
"I'm thinking it will do. But I'll need it for a while until I get back on my feet."
"That's not a problem, going through a rough time?"
"To put it lightly."
"Sorry to hear that pal, it will get better."
"It can't get much worse," I replied.
"You bet your ass it can, remember that. How long you thinking?"
"Maybe a month . . . a little longer, not sure."
"I usually charge eight hundred a month," Tex replied, but for some reason he found a soft spot for me, perhaps because I came across as a completely defeated man who was in dire need of a break. "I could do seven fifty though."

"I can't afford that right now; I can do about six hundred," I replied.

Tex didn't say a word and just stared, trying to gauge my sincerity. Even though Tex was as hard as ice on Pluto, he had a big heart and could feel the depths of pain in my voice. My desperation pierced his armor.

"I can do six."

"Do you take checks?"
"Cash. And I'm not talking about the guy who sang at San Quentin either. And I got three rules: no drugs, no hookers, and pay on time."

I just smiled and came to the conclusion that the check in process was nothing more than a hand shake and a stern warning, It was obvious that there was no credit card machine or towel service here.

"Do you have a map of the grounds?" I joked.
"Yeah, they're at the concierge desk, right next to the valet," Tex cracked back.
This time there was no illustrious anecdote behind the car with the check engine light gleaming brighter than Rudolph's nose, now parked out in front of the third cabin from the left. No underworld spy, no one who's face is on a wanted poster, no bank robber running from the long arm of the law. Nope, this time it was just some poor bastard down on his luck, trying to pick up the pieces of his shattered life.

As I walked back to my car and retrieved the three boxes containing the remnants of what was, and what would never be, I noticed the flagpole with a brightly colored American flag blowing in the wind. I stopped for a brief moment as the long lost feeling of pride came over me, a feeling that my ex wife had taken from me after years of brow beating; she'd also robbed me of my happiness . . . along with my testicles. As I opened the rear passenger door to grab the boxes, a realization came to me. Everything I had perceived as valuable had no value anymore. A lifetime of purchasing random items to make my house a home meant nothing now, but there was plenty of storage in my heart for the free and priceless aspects of life. I placed the strap of my old, tattered leather bag that has been loyal to me since the days of college, over my shoulder and grabbed the box containing the coffee maker, backgammon set and a few albums, and began to trudge my way to the cabin. After about three steps I concluded that the uneven mixture of dirt and rocks were a prime recipe for a twisted ankle, an experience that I wanted strongly to avoid at this juncture. So I redirected my attention to the ground that resembled the lunar surface, instead of the items in the box. After I had traversed though the dirt, I climbed up onto the uneven farmer's porch covered in outdoor carpet. Re-entering the cabin, now breaking a sweat, I looked up to confirm that Tex's interpretation of air conditioning was a fan in the middle of the cathedral ceiling. I placed the box on the kitchen counter and flicked the light switch near the door. The fan began to move as if in a country western film where the fan's only function is to swirl cigar smoke emerging from a group of card cheats below. Furthermore, as if the speed - or lack there of - wasn't enough, the fan wobbled an inch and a half at the completion of every rotation. "With any luck it will fall on my head and put me out of my misery" I said to myself. I brought the rest of the boxes in and started to unpack my woeful life onto the peeling linoleum countertop.

I plugged the coffee maker into the outlet and, not trusting the tint in the water coming from the faucet, removed a bottle from my bag and poured it in. This was not an act of aristocratic behavior, just one of self-preservation. With my luck, I'll be the first person to get Montezuma's revenge in Rhode Island, I told myself.

The aroma of a strong Italian blend coffee soon replaced the smell of dampness. It bothered me that I hadn't purchased whole beans but the grinder didn't make the cut during the move because my ex had bought it for me one birthday, and I didn't want anything from her when starting anew. While the aromas exchanged places, I situated the record player on Chico's table. I pondered for a moment what song was suitable at this particular time. Sam Cooke will do. Yes, Sam Cooke is a good choice because "a change is going to come."

I poured myself a cup and walked out onto the porch. There I sat in the wooden chair listening to Sam's message. For the first time in a long while it felt safe to be myself; there were no eggshells that I needed to tip toe around. I began to cry, not a few tears rolling down my cheek, but streaming waterworks that rivaled old European women who threw themselves on the caskets of loved ones lost, my bellowing continuing for sometime. But as with everything in existence, there was a beginning and an end. What followed was an anomaly; away went the feeling of being a worthless loser. In came the demand to toughen the fuck up! You're strong. You'll get through this! She will look back one day with regret, she doesn't hold that power over you anymore.

For the first time since she had walked out on me, I started to look at what was good about my predicament. I realized that I hadn't lost a wife; I'd lost a toxic human being that didn't deserve to be in the same room with me. I hadn't lost my children; rather I'd gained quality time with them, without my ex running interference. I hadn't lost my house; rather I had left a wooden structure that needed new windows and the lawn cut. I hadn't lost wealth; I'd lost numbers on paper that was supplied by the bank. I finally came to the conclusion that those numbers didn't make me the man I was, and that I would have the opportunity to make more. I had traded all those aspects of my life for peace of mind and solitude; it started to seem like a good exchange. I stood up and slapped myself in the face. "You will survive!" I yelled out loud. Deciding to go for a long distance run, I went in and changed into my running clothes.

CHAPTER 4

·✦·

Always a Straight Shooter

AFTER THE FIRST night, I scrubbed every inch of the cabin and pulled up the musty green carpet to expose wide plank hardwood floors that had been in hiding for the past thirty years. I purchased flooring wax and brought them back to life. I also bought bed sheets along with pillows due to the fact I prefer the feel of cotton on my skin vs. that of the thirty-grit sandpaper that the previous sheets felt like. I purchased the twenty-dollar gallon of paint so desperately needed and painted the dark paneling eggshell white. Last but not least, I replaced the toilet seat, another twenty dollar investment that not only provided a new seat, but also piece of mind every time I sat down to think. The cabin now smelled like a pine tree car freshener rather than mildew.

Two weeks had past since I'd begun to adjust to my new living arrangement. Tex started to visit some mornings for a cup of coffee and to listen to Elvis on the record player, only Elvis. I soon realized that Tex was a great man and began to understand why the cottages were in such a sad state of disrepair. It was a scenario that I would have never imagined. More than one of our conversations revolved around taxation and big government getting in the way of the working man. Tex had purchased the cottages after the war and sustained a living for a while until the government decided to build a highway through the country, a move that destroyed small town America. Instead of stopping for gas and food at mom and pop businesses, travelers became seduced by convenience, filling up and eating at rest stops along the throughway. That, along with the government providing incentives to build cookie cutter condos in the nineteen eighties, had nearly cost Tex the property.

"Americana lost out to affordable convenience," he said. Tex went on to say that when he first bought the cottages there was one other motel in town. Then a dozen high rises appeared out of the ground like giant middle fingers to the ocean.

"It's a god damn shame," he always said at the end of the conversation.

After hearing several of these stories, I began to realize that it was financial, not purposeful neglect that caused the cottages to look so decrepit, and knowing this, somehow made me feel better about my subpar living conditions.

One evening Tex could hear Merle Haggard through his open window. He looked out and saw the storm door open and that the screen door had been replaced on my cabin. Being that it was a beautiful spring night, he grabbed a bottle of whiskey and walked over, knocked on the wood next to the screen and saw me sitting at Chico's table writing a letter.

"Who you writing to?" he asked through the screen.
"My kids, just letting them know how much I love them."

I often wrote letters to my children because I believe that too much is lost in translation with the new forms of communication. I still use modern communication methods for convenience, but there are no feelings in it. I have always thought that there was something magical about putting ink on paper.

"Got time for a whiskey?"
"Always have time for whiskey," I said, turning over the paper to keep my already conveyed emotions privy to the intended recipient.
Since the shot glasses had been left behind - being another meaningless gift from the ex - I grabbed two coffee mugs and walked out onto the porch.

Having brought the other matching chair from Chico's table outside, I placed the two mugs on the red cooler. Tex poured two fingers worth of whiskey in each.

"It's nice to have someone like you staying here, instead of the usual knuckleheads," Tex said as he raised his glass and made a toast.

"Here's to coincidences."
"Do you think they really exist?" I asked, raising my mug.
"Bet your ass kid. Don't' you?"
"I used to, but I'm not so sure anymore."

"You need to open yourself up; then you'll start seeing them for what they really are," Tex said as he took in a mouthful.

"If you say so," I replied a bit confused.
After the second pour of whiskey into the coffee mug, I noticed the smudge mark on Tex's forearm, remnants of what was once was a legible tattoo.

"What was that?" I asked, still holding my coffee mug and pointing with my index finger.

"Oorah", Tex simply replied.
"Were you a Marine?" I queried, not surprised.
"Still am kid."
"Sorry."
"Don't be, I'm not."
"Can you tell me about the war?" I asked, guessing that the answer would be no.

"What do you want to know?"
I was completely taken aback by Tex's agreement to talk about such a topic, since my uncle had served in the Army during World War II and had never spoken a word of it. Only on the day of his funeral did the family learn of his heroism when a representative from the military showed up and presented my aunt with all of his awards.

"What was it like?"

"It was the best and worst time of my life, if that makes any sense."

"What happened out there?" I pressed further.

Tex told me that he was in the battle of Peleliu in the Pacific theater. Omitting most of the details, Tex did acknowledge that he was part of the first wave of men.

"Pretty bad ass," I intercepted.

"Nah, I wasn't a bad ass, just a scared shitless kid trying to survive. Anyway, I made it out alive, and that's more than I can say for most of the men out there. Some reason God didn't want me."

"Only the good die young."

"True."

"Well, maybe he has a plan for you?"

"I'm getting old kid, he better hurry up with that plan, because I'm not going to be around much longer."

"He probably still doesn't want you. I have a feeling that your not going anywhere for a long while."

"Ha." Tex was compelled to continue.

"You have no idea how many great men – friggin' kids - were lost out there, in such a far away place that I couldn't find if I had a map."

I saw the pain on his face and could hear it in his voice.

"Thanks, honestly . . . thank you."

That's all I could muster up to say, and it was enough. Tex poured some more whiskey, and then changed the subject.

"What's a guy like *you* doing here anyway?"

After taking a swig, I provided the cliff note version of the past year, the lies, the hurt, the cheating, and the fact that my ex was now living with the other man in *my* house, raising *my* kids.

Tex then said something profound that night that I would never forget.

"Thousands of men were slaughtered on that beach that day, millions of miles from their homes, that would love to have your problems, but they were never given a chance."

Tex was generally reserved, but like most warm-blooded men, he liked to talk about women. He told me that the best way to get over a woman was to get under another one. I vowed to take his advice along with one more shot of whiskey and began to understand what Tex meant by coincidences.

He didn't speak much, so by default Tex was a great listener. He would sit on the porch and hear what I had to say, my dreams, my mistakes, future plans and past failures. But the few times Tex did interject himself or his thoughts into the conversation, he spoke the hard truth, and nothing but the truth so help you God.

Tex was about as subtle as a three pound cannon ball catapulting over an open field at ninety miles an hour towards a French soldier's kneecap during the Revolutionary war. He would often bitch about the inequalities in America - and not the kind that African Americans have faced for a few hundred years - though Tex did say on more than one occasion that he owed his life to a African American in his unit.

"One time, we were haulin' ass to get out of the shit, and some bastard hurled a grenade - landed right between us. That crazy son of a bitch stopped dead in his tracks, reversed direction, grabbed that grenade right off the ground and threw it right back at those assholes," Tex said shaking his head with a smile.

No, Tex didn't bitch about being brought to a strange land against your will and beaten if you didn't like your new name, but rather he would voice his opposition to the tax structure and welfare system in this country.

"How could someone who never fought for this country get better health care than someone who did!" he would ask, rhetorically.

He had a point I always thought. Tex didn't mind paying taxes.

"With them I buy civility," he'd say. "But the government doesn't have a revenue problem; it has a spending problem. How could a nation give billions of dollars to countries that hate us while we have homeless people here!"

I quickly learned not to bring up that subject again but soon also discerned that Tex loved his country, but was displeased with his government. I could always depend on Tex to give his brutally honest assessment of each situation.

One day I asked, "Why can't I get over her?"
"Most likely because you're a pussy."
"Thanks Tex, I needed that."
"Well, you're not questioning life right now kid, life is questioning you. It's up to you on how you answer it.
Tex's favorite line – at least with me - was one that his instructor in boot camp used to yell at the recruits:
"You better un-fuck yourself, because the world isn't going to do it for you."

Once again, he was honest as a compass. Tex was always right on target though, whether it was in regards to the government giving billions away, or why I couldn't get my ex out of my mind. Those piercing steel blue eyes with crows' feet as deep as the river Nile, didn't lie.

CHAPTER 5

——— ⚜ ———

More - or Less Misty Eyed

ONE SATURDAY MORNING Tex visited cabin number three for some freshly brewed coffee and Elvis live from Hawaii. That night, he told me he was going down the street to the VFW for their annual pig roast.

"Come with me; it will be good for you."

"Nah, no thanks."

"Have you been out since your pity party started?"

I grinned. The reply was "no."

"I'm not taking no for an answer. It's all good people and the food will be great. I'll pick you up at nineteen hundred hours."

"What time is that?" I asked.

"Seven, seven pm" Tex said, as he shook his head and referred to me as a half of a man.

Tex told me that his father had told him that "nothing good is open after midnight besides a woman's legs and a gin joint, both of which only bring trouble." I soon figured out that Tex didn't share his father's ethos.

At six pm, I was feeling depressed and was definitely hesitant about attending, but knew that Tex would never let me stay home. I felt that I had always battled depression. It was certainly lurking around that dark corner of my mind now, but tonight I vowed to be stronger than my thoughts. I defeated the depression that had been so prevalent for the past several months, put on my cleanest pair of dirty jeans and a button down shirt with the least amount of wrinkles. Throwing on my favorite worn out Boston Red sox baseball cap, I walked out onto my porch to avert the need for Tex's summoning.

I wasn't quite sure what to expect when we pulled up at the local VFW for their annual pig roast, but the parking lot didn't disappoint. It was full of American made pick up trucks adorned with American flags, NRA and several yellow "Don't tread on me" bumper stickers. The small, brick building was situated about a hundred feet off the street and it appeared that the same person that paved the cottage drive must have worked (or not!) on this parking lot as well. One solid, windowless, steel door allowed those who dared, to enter the structure. Tex opened the door and was greeted as if he was a cast member of Cheers. Half of the inhabitants of the place yelled his name while the other half hooted and whistled. Not only was Tex a regular, but also the legends of his heroism and valor honored his entrance.

The bar was exactly what I had expected it to be. There were about twenty black, old bar stools with faux vinyl cushioned backs to them. Tex automatically walked to the far left corner of the bar and grabbed the last two seats that were underneath the keno screen. The interior was decorated with a mixture of beer signs and patriotic pictures. On the wall next to us hung a picture of the twin towers with "God bless America" handwritten in big, bold letters above it, and "Never forget" beneath. There was a pool table in the far corner that was being used by a couple of young men. Behind them, a flag with forty-eight stars hung on the wall. I was taking in the surroundings when the bartender came over and placed a bottle of Bud on the bar in front of Tex.

"What are you having, sugar?"

Assuming that the red wine came in either a jug or a cardboard box, I ordered the same as Tex, and thanked her.

As she walked away, along with the rest of the old men sitting at the bar, I checked out her rump. She had on a pair of faded blue jeans from a department store that probably sold everything from lingerie to bicycles. She didn't strike me as the kind of girl who would spend a few hundred dollars on designer clothes, and truth be told, she didn't need to, because her ass was perfect in the ones she had on. She had on a pair of weathered cowgirl boots and a tight fitting T-shirt that read "Peace through superior firepower." Standing about 5'7", she was weight proportionate, and hid her neglected reddish hair under a baseball hat - the kind of girl who considered putting her hair in a pony tail as "doing her hair". As she walked back with the beer I had ordered, I made eye contact with her hazel green eyes. Her eyes exuded a combination of true grit and sexiness. Those eyes told people that she wouldn't hurt them, but not to fuck with her either.

"You like the Red Sox?" I asked.

"No, I like the Yankees but wear this Red Sox hat to throw everyone off," she said with a sarcastic charm that only she could pull off to a perfect stranger. She tipped the brim of her pink Red sox cap and walked over to the two men who were waiting at the bar.

A few minutes later she came back over and introduced herself.

"I'm Misty. You must be the sad sack that Tex told me all about."

I just looked at Tex and shook my head.

"I guess that's me. I'm Hemingway, James Hemingway."

"What a great name, you related to the author?"

"Yup. He was my great uncle. Met him several times and actually have a signed first edition of <u>Farewell to Arms.</u>

"Impressive" Misty said as she walked away, clearly not believing a word that had just come out of my mouth. She came back over a little while later with two more beers that we hadn't ordered. She smiled at me, revealing a few laugh lines that she could care less about. It was refreshing to see a confident woman who was Botox and make-up free.

"Do you want a Sippy cup for this one?"

There was no grey area with Misty. For better or for worse, people knew exactly where she stood on most topics: "So Tex tells me that you're thinking about removing your balls from the mason jar and reattaching them soon. Is that true?"

"Ha!" exclaimed Tex, as he nearly spit out his beer.
"I'm trying ma'am, but it's difficult," I replied.
"Don't ma'am me," Misty said, and then posed another question:
"Does the light make the star, or does the darkness that surrounds it make the star?"

Having no idea what she meant, I answered, "I have no clue."
"Exactly, neither do I," she exclaimed, "but what I do know is that it's the blackness - the nothingness - between the stars is what makes them shine so bright. Without that blackness, those stars could never shine. The emptiness is just as important and as beautiful as the light. So take that pitch black emptiness that you have in your life right now, and understand that it is necessary to make your star shine bright."

I digested what Misty had said as I stared at her derriere saunter away to wait on others. It was then that I noticed a group of young men, barely old enough to vote, sitting at a table in the corner. All were covered in tattoos and one was wearing a pair of tan cargo shorts, revealing a prosthetic leg. I marveled at the number of war stories they were able to trade with the old timers sitting at the table next to them.

Tex and I drank several beers and ate way too much food during the roast. There was no good reason to eat another piece of that cornbread, I had said to myself as I shoveled another piece into my mouth. Tex caught Misty's eye and raised his hand to draw an imaginary check in the air to signify that he wanted the bill. We both reached into our pockets, mine in the front, Tex's in the rear to retrieve his overstuffed wallet. An argument ensued as to who was going to pay the tab. I lost and Tex swore at me, correction - I was the son, my mother was called a bitch.

As we were getting up to leave the equivalent of ocean front property at a bar, Misty walked over and asked why we were leaving so early?

"My dad needs to get home," I said, finally getting one shot in.
"Screw you." Tex replied.
"Do *you*?" asked Misty, staring directly at me.
"Umm, no, not really, but he's my ride home." I stammered back.
"Well then I suggest you sit back down Darling, and have another drink so you can help me clean this joint when these boys leave. I'll get you home safe."

Tex, being the great wingman that he was, picked up on what Misty was saying. "Good night you two. Don't do anything I wouldn't do," he said to Misty as he winked at me behind her back, and walked out.

Now that I didn't have Tex to converse with and Misty was busy flirting with all the old vets, I turned my attention to the

Jason Felix DeCesare

war movie that was playing on the old projection television. The volume was off and the subtitles were on, though no one needed to read what was being said as Chuck Norris rescued POWs. Misty intermittently checked on me. Each time we engaged in a quick, light conversation. At one point I almost invited her to dinner but then thought better of it. "I guess my balls are still in that Mason jar, I admitted to myself." Before I knew it, closing time had arrived. Misty put her thumb and pointer finger in her mouth and whistled as loudly as a train crossing an intersection, followed by a "last call boys. You don't have to go home, but you can't stay here!"

I was feeling the dozen or so stubbies I had ingested and my self- defeatist attitude reared its ugly head, as it so often did of late.

"What the hell are you thinking - she doesn't want you. You're a train wreck. Just walk home now and save yourself the embarrassment," my inner voice chastised as she was clearing beer bottles off a table.

Misty walked over and provided an unnecessary apology for not engaging me during the night. Having seen how very busy she'd been, I responded,
"No worries, you had your hands full."
"I'm going to leave now Misty. It was so nice meeting you."
"Really? Why?"
"Well, I just don't want to be a bother to you. I can walk home; it's not that far," even though I knew it *was* that far.

44

"Don't be ridiculous Hemingway. You're not going anywhere. Now put those chairs on top of those tables."

I walked past the 1980's neon jukebox that was playing "Fortunate Son" by Credence Clearwater Revival and began to complete the chore Misty had assigned.. The only table on which I didn't place the chairs, was still occupied by three of the young men with short cropped haircuts and tattoos, with only five legs among them. Misty knew all of them by first name, and only had to tell them once to finish up. They all stood and put the chairs they'd been sitting in on top of the table, a step that I realized was completely unnecessary because at no point was a vacuum cleaner ever going to pass underneath that or any other table prior to tomorrow's opening. After they had all placed their respective chairs on the table, the soldier with the prosthetic leg drunkenly asked Misty if he could get a kiss good night. As soon as the sentence finished slurring out of his mouth, his buddies grabbed him and headed towards the door. Misty quickly replied no, and that if he kept it up she would take his leg and throw it into the parking lot, call the cops and have them issue a summons for littering! They all busted out laughing, including the one missing the leg.

"Once you go one, you're all done!" he yelled out. "I love you Misty!"
"I love you too Joshua," she called back, as she saluted them walking towards the door. They stopped in mid stride, snapped to attention and returned the salute.

"At ease boys, and get home safe," she said sincerely.

I walked back and sat on the stool located at the center of the bar. Misty had her back to me as she grabbed the old silver champagne bucket right next to the register that was being used as a tip jar. Again, I caught myself looking at her rear end, this time noticing the dime sized hole above her right pocket. She's either cut out the middle-man or she's wearing thongs I surmised, both scenarios suiting me just fine. Misty looked at me through the mirror that was behind the bar and caught me checking her out.

"Take a picture; it will last longer."

Hearing I'd been caught, I smiled and apologized. She smiled in the affirmative. Misty turned around, tipped the champagne bucket over and let her hard-earned money fall onto the bar in front of me.

"Could you count this for me, while I count the drawer?"
"Sure."

She grabbed two of my least favorite beers and opened them. I didn't care though; I would have drunk motor oil if it helped my chances with Misty. Who was I to complain to a woman with a hole in her tight fitting jeans wearing a Red Sox cap, who seemed more than remotely interested in me. We counted our money separately, but together, and as if the heavens opened and down ascended the goddess of sexual innuendos to count the money herself, the total came to sixty nine dollars.

"Sixty nine," I said with just the faintest smirk.

"Keep dreaming," she chided, as she put the pile of assorted bills in her pocket. Their eyes connected once again, as she smiled and said,

"You're all right, Hemingway."

"You're not too shabby yourself Misty," I replied sheepishly but unable to contain my grin. Misty chugged the last half of her beer and informed me that we were leaving. I followed suit, quickly finishing my beer as well.

Misty called, "let's go Alice," as she walked out from behind the bar and made her way to the door, asked me to hit the lights on the wall, and then waited for me. Once we were both outside, she turned and locked the solid steel door. The only vehicle left in the parking lot was a white pick up truck with a pink NRA sticker in the rear window.

"No shit," I said out loud. I wasn't sure where I stood on the issue of the NRA and gun control, but now certainly wasn't the time to have an intelligent discussion on the matter. Serious conversations were intended for rotundas and wives, not with perspective one-night stands while half drunk.

"Just skim the surface," I reminded myself.

As soon as she turned the ignition, Patsy Cline's "I go Walking after Midnight" came on the tape deck and our small talk continued. Apparently she had made the decision to take me to her place without informing me, seeing that she never asked me where I lived as we pulled out of the dirt parking lot. After a ten-minute drive, we arrived at her condo. The complex contained about thirty units and a pool - actually filled with chlorinated water. By the appearance of the cars in the lot, this was a workingman's place to live, a place where people put in an honest workweek and didn't live above their means.

As we exited the truck, Misty told me to be quiet so as not to wake up her son.

"Oh, o.k." I replied, a bit stunned by this newly, acquired information. Misty was fumbling with her keys while we were standing on the front steps when the door suddenly opened.

"Hey mom", the boy said rubbing his blue, teenage eyes.
"Hey honey, sorry I woke you." Say hi to mom's friend, Hemingway."
"Hey," he said without a care in the world as to whom the asshole was standing with his mother at three in the morning. Once inside, she gave her son a hug and kiss and walked him upstairs.

"The couch is all yours big boy, make yourself at home."

I stood there for a minute not knowing what to do. Should I leave? But not having any idea where I was or how to get home, I thought better of it. Misty didn't even provide a blanket or pillow for me. "God damn it," I said to myself more than once. I finally sat on the couch and lectured myself with the typical drunk ego-defeating conversation that I was used to having several times a week. I took my button down shirt off and was trying to decide whether to turn it into a blanket or a pillow.

Just as I was calling myself an idiot again I heard the slow, methodical, footsteps of someone trying to strategically place his/her feet so as to not create a sound. I lifted my head from the wooden armrest turned pillow, and saw Misty standing at the end of the stairs. This time she wasn't wearing her jeans and baseball cap. She had changed into a men's extra large T-shirt that hung off her shoulder and ended right below her crotch, revealing beautiful, milky white skin. Most likely a remnant from the last man that was here in the exact same position that I was, but again, this was no time to judge.

She walked over and without saying a word, straddled me and began to kiss my neck. Apparently, foreplay was not her forte, she quickly removed my pants and underwear with the precision of a Special Forces operation. As she continued to kiss me, she reached down with one of her hands and stroked me until I was hard. She then grabbed my penis and put it inside her wet and willing self. Still shocked at the quickness in which I was finally getting laid, I soon came to the realization that Misty was very good at the art of having sex discreetly. I hoped that her being muffled was due to her son sleeping a few feet above us, separated only by a thin layer of drywall, and not due to my performance.

I had never worried about my performance or size during my marriage, but with the discovery of Internet porn, I'd been wondering if I might be inadequate. I had heard that the camera added ten pounds but did it add five inches as well? "One guy's package was so long, it needed an elbow," I had jokingly reported to one of my male co-workers over lunch.

Misty appeared as if she was very pleased but the lingering feelings of self-doubt still persisted. She moved up and down while on top of me with grace and skill, then grabbed my hand and put it on the ass that I had stared at all night, so I started squeezing it. Apparently that was not what she wanted, because she took my hand and guided it inside. "Holy shit!" but again, who was I to argue with a woman who knew exactly what she wanted in order to achieve an orgasm? As soon as I inserted my finger, her excitement intensified. She moaned and began to ride me much harder and faster. "Don't stop," she told me. With there only being a thin layer of skin separating the two orifices, I could feel my penis inside her with my finger. Was it possible to be completely creeped out and turned on at the same time? My wife made it very clear in the beginning of our ill- fated relationship that her ass was "exit only." What a great example of the cliché that variety might indeed be the spice of life. We orgasmed at nearly the same time, which was followed by a peck on the lips by Misty. She lay in contented stillness for a few minutes, but eventually got off of me as gingerly as she had gotten on, walked up the stairs in the same fashion she had descended, and disappeared.

I stood and found the bathroom on the first floor near the couch. I went for two reasons, first to wash my finger, and second to urinate. I scrubbed the finger like a doctor does pre-op. and smelled it several times to insure its cleanliness. "Why the hell would I smell it?" I laughed to myself, while smelling it yet again. I lay back down and played back the events of what had just occurred. I was proud of my performance, but for some reason felt guilty, as if having sex somehow distanced me from my ex. My eyes grew heavy as I pulled up my long sleeved shirt that I'd decided to use as a blanket, lifting it to the bottom of my chin, and quickly fell asleep.

I awoke way too early due to a conversation that was taking place at the kitchen table in the next room. Ugh, my head. *Oh God, what have I done?* And **what** am I doing here? I admonished myself the second I realized I was in a stranger's house. I bolted upright immediately and with my unstable equilibrium, checked for my wallet, keys and cell phone, all of which were in place. Misty noticed that I was awake and beckoned me to join them for breakfast. I walked into the kitchen to find her in the same T-shirt, but noticed that she was wearing a bra underneath and a pair of SpongeBob flannel bottoms. I sat at the small table, anguishing over the awkwardness I could have cut with a dull spoon, not from Misty, but from her teenage son who was glaring at me from across the table. The son didn't make a sound, but his look said everything. Does he know? Could he hear us? *Get me out of here*, my squeamish innards screamed. Misty made pancakes straight from a box whose label read "just add water." I ate in the dreaded silence. She finally explained to her son that I was her old friend from the Army and had been too drunk to drive home. Hopefully the kid bought it.

"Oh really?" the son asked. "What unit?" Not knowing anything about the military, I dumbly replied, "Uh, the Army." Luckily Misty's son dropped the subject and asked for another serving of rubbery pancakes. Awkward small talk about his high school football team ensued. We finally finished eating breakfast and I helped Misty clear the paper plates and put them in the trash.

"Lets go cupcake," she said, not in an endearing way, but rather with sarcasm, as she grabbed the keys from the brass hook next to the door.

"It was nice meeting you," I said to her son who just nodded his head in acknowledgment.

On the drive home awkward silence permeated the air, only to be interrupted by even more awkward conversation on my behalf. I had always been a complete gentleman but hadn't had to experience a morning like this for so long that I had no idea what to say. I told Misty where I lived and thankfully, it was rather close. As she pulled up to the cabins, we said our good byes and nice meeting you's, then she drove off. I never asked for her number and she never offered it; perfect . . . I guess.

As soon as I'd entered cabin number three, I took a long, lukewarm shower with low water pressure and crawled back into bed to sleep my headache away. I had my visitation later on that evening for a few hours and didn't want to appear hung-over. 'Visitation' I thought - sounds like something a person in prison is granted, not a loving parent.

The following weeks were uneventful. I went to work, spent some time with my children, and had my balls busted by my ex. I woke up to an email one morning informing me that I owed her twelve dollars and fifty cents, for half of a twenty-five dollar co-pay. I paid three hundred dollars a week for my children and in addition, gladly paid for my oldest to take yoga classes, never asking my ex for a cent. The email was sent at 6:32 am. "Who the hell sends an email like that at 6:32am?" I asked no one in particular. I was beginning the see that her leaving was the best thing that could have happened to me. I had lacked the courage to leave and had sincerely wanted to raise my children as a family, so much so that - at times - I had begged her to work things out. Perhaps such an unanswered prayer is God's way of showing us how delusional our request was to begin with.

I informed Tex of my transgressions when he visited that morning for his usual coffee and Elvis.

"Good for you, did you get to meet her son?"
"Holy shit! How do you know?"
"He's a good kid, hell of a football player. You're not the only one that has been to her place kid," he added. I didn't inquire if Tex was referring to himself or other patrons, or both. Some things are better off not knowing.

CHAPTER 6

─── ⚜ ───

Global Warming and Cats

"I MIGHT SET up a social media account today. Everyone does it and I think it's a great way for people to connect," I told Tex.

"You're crazy. Don't do that."
"Why not?"
"Because it's the antichrist, that's why."
"What is?" I asked confused.
"The Internet, that's who."

Tex had always been a religious man but he didn't pigeon-hole his beliefs into one category. He was a very spiritual student of history, a history rich with omens and coincidences. He went on to opine that, "Since the beginning of time, people have created an antichrist. Every religion – in every region of the world – there has always been one individual who was labeled as the antichrist. Maybe it was a dictator, a president, an opposing ruler or a musician. But it's *not* a person; one person could never harness the ability to destroy all of humanity. A thousand years ago, a ruler, a king, or a priest would yell from his ivory tower and spread the word of an antichrist. It would conceivably reach a few thousand people, maybe a whole region, but the Internet can reach the entire population with one push of a button. The Internet and social media have the power to destroy and they are doing so. Look at all the death and destruction the spreading of hate has caused, all the cheating, pornography etc. - it's all there. It's the melting pot for the demise of the human race. A million Hitler's could never do what the Internet has done. How do you think half of these wars and uprisings have occurred lately? Think about it."

"Do you honestly believe that?

"Yup, and trust me, if you think for one second that the government doesn't watch everything that you have ever typed, you're highly mistaken. They even have the ability to spy on your key strokes, not just your searches."

As off-center as I'd thought Tex was before he'd articulated his theory, he once again made me question whether my assumptions and beliefs had been thought through thoroughly enough. I heeded Tex's warning and decided against the creation of an online social media account, but I still surfed for the occasional girl on girl porno. I was resigned, however, to meet the woman of my dreams the old fashioned way, perhaps with eye contact while reaching for the same bag of potato chips, or an introduction somewhere other than in a night club or bar.

And that's exactly what happened a week later at a global conglomerate coffee shop, where the person behind the counter usually misspells your name on the side of your cup, and eight dollars gets you a small coffee and a high calorie snack. I noticed an attractive woman standing directly behind me in line. We made eye contact and exchanged the standard salutations. After mulling it over in my head, I worked up the courage to place my hand out.

"I'm Hemingway, James Hemingway. And you are?"
"Hope"
"Very nice to meet you Hope. What are you reading? I asked pointing to the book in her hand.

"It's a book on the environment."

"Great, I love the Earth too," I said, realizing how corny I sounded as soon as the words clumsily rolled off my tongue. I felt more comfortable telling her that I loved her name.

"It's the only good thing to come from Pandora's box."
"Really? What is?"
"Hope. All the ruins of man escaped from the box that day, but so did hope. With hope, the ruins can be defeated, without it, we're all doomed."

"That's fascinating, I never knew that, she replied sincerely."
"Yup, true story."
I was next to order. "May I buy you a coffee, Hope?"

"Um, sure, thanks," she said as she began to order a mixture of various ingredients as if creating a potion.

"The girl behind the counter must have a degree in physics," I said to Hope, while I ordered a simple small black.

I paid for both coffees and Hope thanked me more than once for my generosity. I grabbed my small, rudimentary black as she took possession of her chemistry experiment, and found a table outside on the small concrete deck. It was sectioned off from the parking lot by a black, rod iron fence, just close enough to the local traffic so patrons could taste the exhaust while their skin absorbed the nutrients provided by the sun. As the conversation progressed, Hope disclosed that she was the editor of a local newspaper focused on climate change.
"Don't you mean global warming?"
"Yes, same thing," she said.
"Well, don't you think it was rebranded in order to explain the freezing cold winters?"

Her answer surprised me. "Yes, I guess you could say that, but you can't deny that climate change is real; look at the storms, the rising of the oceans, the melting of the polar caps."

"You're right. I don't deny their existence either, but I disagree on the cause, that's all. I think it's a natural progression of the ebb and flow of the universe and not man-made. I make an effort to recycle and I'm conscience of my carbon footprint, but my riding a bike for six miles to work won't change a thing, especially when the people telling me to ride my bike to work, fly private jets all over the place dumping thousands of gallons of jet fuel into the atmosphere. I just think that they are hypocrites getting rich off of an industry, that's all."

Hope rattled off several statistics about the earth's temperature and conditions that needed to be addressed. I agreed with all, but just thought that mankind wasn't to blame.

"I just don't think man is that powerful to affect the outcome of temperature; we're giving ourselves way to much credit."

Hope completely disagreed with my assessment on the topic and informed me of my idiocy and ignorance.

"Ouch," I replied. Why can't I have a different opinion than you? I'm not mad at you for blaming man. Why are you mad at me for blaming evolution? I drive a car that gets thirty-one miles to a gallon. They drive in motorcades laden with SUV's. I fly once every five years to Florida on a commercial plane while they take private jets every week, that's all I'm trying to say. I apologize if I offended you."

"It's because of people like you that the Earth is going to die," she persisted.

"Me? I go out of my way not to step on an ant, and I'll have you know that when I catch bugs in my house, I actually release them. Now I'm being accused of killing a whole planet? Trust me Hope, we are nothing more than an irritation on the Earth's surface, and when it doesn't want us here anymore, I'm sure we will be the first ones to know."

I began to feel the tension mounting in my chest and knowing that feeling was toxic, decided it was time to graciously thank Hope for her time and walk away. I knew I would never be able to repair the damage that had been done, so I stood up from the table, told her it was a pleasure meeting her and did exactly that, trying to figure out what the *hell* had just happened.

The next morning over coffee, I told Tex what had happened on the prior day. "I know better never to ask a woman her age or weight, but I knew nothing of this global warming stuff! I would have been better off asking her if she was pregnant!"

"Some women are very sensitive," Tex replied.
"Sensitive? She accused me of murdering the planet. That's about as sensitive as an automatic flushing toilet, you know, the ones that flush every time you cough or sneeze, and soak your undercarriage."

Tex laughed, "Never thought of it that way, but yes, you're right."
"Not to change the subject, but to change the subject, I said, I've got a date next weekend."

"Good for you, glad to see you back in the saddle," Tex said, as he took a mouthful of black coffee.

The time came for my date and, unlike the night I met Misty, I opted to wear a clean shirt without *any* wrinkles. We had made plans earlier in the day to meet at a restaurant in town at eight pm. I wasn't thrilled about the location because it was the type of place where one has to spend twenty-six dollars for a piece of chicken. Hopefully this meet and greet didn't involve said chicken, but rather a cocktail and salted bar nuts. I arrived at quarter of eight and took a seat at the granite bar. At three past eight, I received a text message.

"I'm running a lil late, sry lol."
Unlike the sender of the message, the recipient was not "laughing out loud."

I took a deep breath while the bartender poured me a twelve-dollar glass of wine from a bottle I had purchased earlier in the week for sixteen at the store. The drink arrived and extracted a long awaited sip. As I looked at my watch and noticed that it was twenty-eight minutes past the hour and still no sign of my date, I felt someone tap on my opposite shoulder, making me look in the wrong direction, a move that would usually have amused me a bit, but her tardiness had soured my humor.

"Hemingway?"

"Yes."

"Oh hi, so nice to finally meet you, sorry I'm late."

Her apology was as dry as the fourteen-dollar martini she ordered. I couldn't help but think of what my father in law had said the day of my open bar wedding: "All beer drinkers become scotch drinkers when someone else picks up the tab."

Still the gentleman, I never mentioned the fact that she was thirty minutes late, ruining the only opportunity she'd had to make a great first impression. At first glance, she appeared very attractive with a nice figure but my impression was that she was more aware of her beauty than I was. She was well spoken and gainfully employed by a banking institution. The second character flaw I observed was the fact that she finished her martini before I finished the wine I had ordered thirty minutes prior. We continued with small talk and ordered two more of the same. At least she isn't ordering the chicken, I thought to myself. She told me about her passion for cats and how she volunteered at the animal shelter. I could tolerate cats but was by no means fond of them. I thought that the very idea of an animal shitting in a box down the hall, and then walking on the countertops and kitchen table was disgusting. This opinion I decided to keep to myself, having learned my lesson from the global warming debacle with Hope. Ms. Feline described how she set out traps to catch strays in order to spay or neuter them to help control the population.

"Wow, I had no idea you could even do that, that's great," I said, hoping that my approval and feigned interest in the uninteresting topic, might increase my odds of seeing her naked.

She told me several stories that revolved around her three cats and the time she spent working at the shelter, so I decided to contribute the only cat story I knew to the conversation. I told her about the time I'd visited Ernest Hemingway's house several years prior when vacationing in Key West.

"Oh my god, are you related to him?"
"No, I wish. I can't even write a Christmas card, let alone a novel."
"You're funny Hemingway."
"Thanks, but sadly enough, I've only read one of his books, and that was only because it was a required reading in high school. Anyways, the house was beautiful and had a large stonewall surrounding the property and probably a few hundred cats that lived there. They all have an extra hove, or claw, or . . . what do you call their feet?"

"A paw?"
"Yes, paw; they all have an extra toe on their paw."
"What do you mean they have a few hundred cats?"
"Well, I'm sure I'm exaggerating, but there were a lot of cats walking around the property. You could pet them and

everything. If you like cats, you'd love it there," I relayed innocently, not knowing that what I'd just said would tip off a downward spiral.

"No, that's ridiculous. You can't have that many cats on one property! That must be against the ordinance of the town. Who takes care of these cats? Are they spayed? It's an absolute violation to let that many cats wander around one property," she admonished, completely incensed.

Literally taken aback on my bar stool, I responded, "Look, I have no idea what the city ordinance is for the town of Key West, and I'm sure the cats are well taken care of. I really couldn't care less about the cats at Hemingway's house. I was just making small talk by telling you the only cat story I knew. There's no reason for you to get so upset."

"I'm not upset at you. It's just that those cats are being mistreated and they should not be allowed to house that many cats on the property. That's why every town in America has ordinances in place."

Overwhelmed by her hostility, I countered, "I don't want to come across as heartless but I couldn't care less about those cats. I was just trying . .

"What do you mean you don't care about cats!" she clawed back, interrupting.

"That's not what I said; you put words in my mouth. All I'm saying is that I tried to tell you a nice story, the only story I had that involved cats - I thought you'd enjoy it. There was no reason for you to get so agitated."

"There's just no way that they are allowed to have a hundred cats on one property. I am absolutely contacting that city hall on Monday to see what the ordinance is, and to see how it's possible for them to get away with that."

At that, I stood up and reached into my pocket, removed forty dollars and said, "Good luck with your investigation, it was very nice meeting you, but this is over the top for me."

"You're seriously leaving?" she asked, with the same astonished look I'd had just minutes ago on my face.

"Yes. You may be very nice but you're not for me. You need to find someone that shares your fervent concern about feline well-being. Good bye."

I didn't even consider shaking her hand because that could easily have prolonged the dreadful conversation. I figured that my forty dollars wouldn't cover the whole tab, but it was enough for my drinks, plus one of hers, and that was plenty. As I was walking out I looked at my watch: nine twenty three. It had taken less than one hour for that date to implode, I mused. As I was pulling out of the parking lot, I noticed her getting into a car that was parked in a handicapped parking spot.

"God, she sucks. That wasn't nice, I'm sorry." I said as I immediately apologized to the universe.

I couldn't wait until the next coffee and Elvis session with Tex. I was actually looking forward to his brutal assessment of my date. Tex always seemed to bring levity to the depressing predicament that was my life. That weekend Tex didn't fail to deliver when I went into detail about the cat lady.

CHAPTER 7

———— ⚜ ————

Be Grateful

"Cats? Who would have thought! I love cats," said Tex.

"You do?" Hemingway asked, surprised.

"Yeah, with barbecue sauce," he replied sarcastically.

"Ha! I prefer teriyaki on mine," I said.

"She really parked in a handicapped space? What an awful human being. That's enough information to never speak to her again. Who does that? It's the little things that show one's character. All the little things add up to the totality of one's character. I would rather take a person on a date that was on parole for shoplifting than have my date park in a handicapped spot. Should have pissed in her gas tank."

"Didn't have time," I said. "I just wanted to get the hell away from her."

"One of the ways to gauge character is how you act when no one is watching," Tex replied.

I voiced my frustration with not being able to meet a good woman.

"Ok, so I can't talk about weight, age, global warming and cats now. When did this list grow? I never knew that the list could be extended. It was always just weight and age!"

Tex, always being the unrefined one, replied, "Hemingway, you better un fuck yourself. Go ask Joe McCarthy if you should be depressed after a few shitty dates."

"Who? I don't know a Joe McCarthy."
"Exactly. You wouldn't know him you asshole, because he died in my arms when he was only nineteen years old. All McCarthy used to talk about was all the chicks he was going to date when he got back home. He loved them all, but he was cut down one day and never got the chance. He would have loved to be sitting there listening to those ding bats talk about global warming and cats. Trying to find a perfect mate is like finding a unicorn; it's impossible because she doesn't exist. Just try to find one that is less crazy than the last, one that has soft, caring eyes and a big heart that won't cheat on you. But the cheating part is tough to predict because I don't think the person sets out to cheat in the beginning. It just happens when the relationship gets boring; sometimes the one who's cheated on, is just as much to blame as the cheater. When a man treats his wife like an object and ignores her for ten years, I tell you what, kid, someone is going to tell her how beautiful she is and someone's going to buy her those flowers she wanted from her husband. And on the flip side

of the coin, when a wife has a headache five days a week and nags her husband about everything, well, guess what, that woman at the office doesn't have a headache and she's not brow beating him about nonsense. I'm not saying it's right, but that's the hard truth. The whole thing is complicated and screwed up; it's never black and white."

"Never thought of it that way."
"It's all gray kid, the whole fucking world is gray."
 The next few weeks passed by in relative monotony. The sameness of the passing days along with the rising and setting of the sun fatigued me just as it does the masses. Wake up by an annoying alarm, a quick jog, work and sleep, the day perforated by a few cups of coffee and hopefully a decent meal . . . repeat. The next weekend was going to be different however, because I planned to take my children to a small amusement park in New Hampshire. Before the divorce it was always Florida, but with my now limited resources, New Hampshire would have to do. I found a hotel for sixty-nine dollars a night that had cable and served a continental breakfast. Sadly enough, even at that price, it made me nervous to spend that amount of money. I justified spending it because, as Tex put it simply, "Chalk it up to preventative maintenance so your kids don't grow up to be assholes. Better to spend the money on them now as children than on lawyers as they get older." He told me of a story that involved a small kid from his days of being a parent.

"There was a kid who lived across the street whose parents never took him anywhere or paid attention to him."

Tex told me how he could always see the jealousy on the child's face when he learned that Tex's family was going on vacation. Years later Tex read in the paper that same kid was arrested for robbing a bank.

"Now I'm not saying a vacation could've prevented a bank robbery, but I wouldn't take that chance, if I were you."

Friday morning I drove to my old house and noticed a brand new SUV parked beside the one I had purchased for my ex the year before. The front door was already open due to anticipation from my daughters, and as soon as they saw me they came out with controlled excitement. They wanted to run to the car but were governed to walk while holding their mother's hand until all three reached the side of my car. Why did she have to walk them to the car? They were old enough to walk. Was it just another way for her to attempt to control the situation, something she was losing with each passing day. Just as I was becoming annoyed, I looked at my ex wife's face and noticed that there was something different about it. I couldn't quite place what it was, but something was different. What is it? I kept asking myself. As the not knowing was occupying my mind, the kids jumped into the car with unhinged enthusiasm. "Daddy, I'm so excited, " the oldest one said. "Me too!" yelled the little one just as loud, but at a higher pitch.

As we started our journey to New Hampshire, my ex's face kept troubling me. What was it? Holy shit, that's it; it's her lips. She got fake lips! Oh my God, she looks absurd; who is she trying to fool? How could she possibly believe that it looks good - or natural for that matter? It's the woman's version of a toupee or a comb over. You're not fooling anyone; everyone thinks it looks farcical, but they are just being polite by not saying anything. And the men are keeping their mouths shut in hopes of getting laid.

"Well, I guess her outside, matches her insides now, fake," I said under my breath.

"What dad? Did you say something?" my oldest asked.
"Oh, no honey, I was just thinking out loud, that's all."
The kids didn't say much about the ex - or the man that had replaced me faster than it takes a decorator to decide what color to paint a room. When they did share a few stories, I just smiled and said what a good person he must be. It was for the greater good I told myself, even though I would rather have shaved my head with a cheese grater than to hear stories about the man that was now parked in my driveway.

We finally arrived at the motel. It was a two-story motor lodge with a swimming pool, surrounded by the pavement of the parking lot like a stagnant moat around a mid evil castle. "Thank you God, for not allowing my children to realize that their dad is poor; you're a good man," I acknowledged more than once.

We walked into the lobby and I checked in as the two girls wandered around looking at the various mounted animal heads. At the repeated request of the girls, I brought them straight to the pool after I'd put the bags in the room. As soon as I'd opened the chain link fence that separated the cars from the lounge chairs, the girls ran with reckless abandon directly into the water. Whereas Dad, being the typical conservative adult that somewhere along the way, lost his childhood magic, performed the standard test of determining the temperature by running my toes along the top the water.

"Whoa, that's cold. You girls have fun."
"Daddy, please! Come throw us around," the girls pleaded.
I was usually known to be a big kid myself whenever I was with my children in a pool, but the cold New Hampshire air had gotten the best of me. I went and sat in a small, white plastic chair that was part of a table set and read a few brochures I had picked up in the lobby. I then did exactly what any mature adult would do in that situation, ha! Without hesitation, I got up, ran to the edge of the pool and leaped while yelling "cannonball."

The desired effect was achieved, as I soaked both the girls, along with an elderly couple leaning against the edge in waist deep water. The older man laughed while his wife wiped her eyes of the chlorinated water.

"I'm so sorry." I said.

"Don't be, I'd do the same if my knees let me."

After enjoying our time in the pool, all three of us went inside and changed up for dinner, stopping in the lobby to ask the attendant about a good pizza place in town. The man behind the counter handed us another brochure stating that the best pizza in New Hampshire was right down the street. "Perfect," I said, "We love pizza and we're all tired from the drive up and the pool." We piled into the car and headed down the street to find the pizza joint exactly where the man had said it would be. When the pizza arrived, I could tell that the author of that brochure either lied, or that the people of New Hampshire had no clue what a good pizza entailed. The only redeemable quality of the pizza place was that they had installed small independent jukeboxes on the wall next to each table. There, we listened to Johnny Paycheck's "Take this Job and Shove it", Sinatra's "Summer Wind" and "Living and Dying in Three quarters Time," by Jimmy Buffett. Each sounded like it was being played through the broken speaker of a gramophone from a hundred yards away.

The next morning all three of us woke up in the same bed, even though there was a perfectly good empty one on the other side of the night stand. "That bed is for jumping daddy," the little one informed me.

We showered and dressed in record breaking time, ate a quick, surprisingly good continental breakfast in the lobby, and arrived at the amusement park after a twenty minute drive through the mountains. When we arrived, there was already a long line of families waiting at the entrance. I soon realized that I was an unwillingly observant in a relationship experiment that had just begun. My heart grew heavy after the first hour of walking around noticing that I was one of only a few single parents at the park. All I observed was the togetherness of families, walking together, talking together, eating together, even being annoyed together, something I had myself convinced I would never experience again. I felt like I was the only single dad at the park that day, but as soon as I decided to regain control of my thoughts and focus on what was, instead of what would never be, I realized that this day was similar to the morning I had walked out of court. I began to notice that nothing was simply as it appeared. I saw that most of the husbands and wives had a look of discontent on their faces. They walked several feet apart from each other, often using their children as buffer zones. While waiting in line for one of the rides, we stood behind a family where it was blatantly clear that the mother and father had checked out years ago. They wanted nothing more than to be home, sitting on the couch, eating saturated fats while independently looking at their mobile devices to distract them from their misery. As expected, the little boy, filled with anticipation of the coming excitement, stepped up on the bottom rung of the barricade and lifted himself six inches off the ground. Instead of allowing him to be the child that he was, the mother was more interested in correcting every aspect of his behavior. How dare that son bother her while she was reading the latest post on her social network! She wanted a perfect specimen for a child, one with no energy or zest for life, just like herself. "Red light!" she would yell at her son every time he moved. It was awful; I felt so badly for this muted child. Again the kid moved, and again, she yelled "Red light!" As I witnessed one of the saddest displays of parenting skills I had ever observed, I whispered to my girls, "You two have no clue how lucky you are."

That kid will definitely rob a bank when he gets older, I said to myself, half seriously. The mother never spoke with love and affection towards her child, just with commands and orders, while the brow beaten, overweight, oblivious father just played a game on his phone and didn't intervene on behalf of the likewise overweight, brow beaten son. The father had the typical forty pounds of unwanted fat and was aided by a knee brace, most likely due to a minor injury from his glory days of playing high school football, an injury that didn't require surgery then, and certainly not a knee brace now.

"That must be the reason why he didn't make the NFL," I chuckled to myself.

I allowed my kids to be kids while enchantment still filled their hearts, in view of the knowledge that before they knew it, the stressors of life would take over and snuff that magic out. I understood that one day soon I would put my children down for the last time, never to be picked up again, so I enjoyed the innocence while it still existed. So, as a screw you to those miserable parents, I allowed my daughters to step up on the bottom rung of the three pipe fence system whose sole purpose was to herd the people like cattle to the entrance of the ride. I, on the other hand, didn't have a spouse to argue with or be annoyed or ignored by. My children weren't buffer zones or distractions, nor were they convenient excuses not to be intimate. They were the reason for my happiness and why I pulled myself out of bed each morning, the only reason at this point.

Even though loneliness wouldn't leave me alone, I felt complete when around my children. The world seemed to be a better place and all of my stressors and insecurities move to the background of my mind. The rest of the weekend was filled with laughter, empty calories and countless scoops of ice cream. I even allowed the little one to push me in the pool with my T-shirt on, at the amusement of the same older couple that I'd soaked a few days prior. As I pulled into the driveway to drop my children off, I broke the promise I'd made to my daughters and myself. My heart grew heavy and I began to cry. My children gave me kisses, never enough but enough to get me through the week. As they walked themselves through the front door, I drove away thinking that's the front door I will never walk through again; that's the same doorway where I'd been the recipient of countless empty hugs that rang hollow as the liberty bell. I allowed the negative thoughts to enter my soul for the rest of the way home, but could then hear Tex yelling at me to toughen up: "You control those thoughts; they don't control you!" I was determined to win the war, but conceded this particular battle. Where did all those relationships I'd observed this weekend go wrong? Were they in love with each other at one point in time, and it just was a natural progression that they grew apart? Was it the complacency and all the running around to get to those soccer practices and birthday parties? Was it something so simple as the little annoying habits that everyone has that drives the wedge between partners over the years? Was it an unplanned pregnancy where one or both tried to do the right thing for the sake of the child? Relationships could never survive with resentment or anger being a cornerstone.

The next coffee and Elvis session, I allowed myself to open up to Tex. "I don't want to you bitch at me or call me a pussy but I need for you to hear me out."

"You got it kid, and I never bitch at you, I just want you to be strong so you can get though this, that's all."

"I know, and I can't thank you enough for being there for me. I have no one else to talk to but honestly, I have no clue where my marriage went off track. I was a good man Tex. I was home every night cooking dinner and making sure the homework was done. Like most people, I had many faults, but none too big nor too many. I didn't drink too much and was always a gentleman with other woman. I had chances, as everyone does, but never bit that baited hook, and there were a few times where that bait was perfect. I was home every night at a reasonable hour, never smoked and only enjoyed the occasional red wine or Mexican beer. I mean I watched porn once in a while but who the hell doesn't now a day? Christ, I even hate golf. My family never lost a Sunday afternoon to that or football. I always put family first Tex, I swear I did. "God damn it." I said as I threw the rest of my English muffin towards the flagpole in disgust.

"I know kid, life isn't fair, but no where does it say that it's supposed to be. There are all types of injustices in this world, and not to piss you off, but most of them are much bigger than yours.

"I know, I know, my kids are healthy I get it."
"It had nothing to do with you.
"I beg to differ Tex."
"Hear me out, it didn't matter if you bought her one more bouquet or made one more dinner; it didn't matter to her. She didn't cheat on you, she wasn't even thinking about you. You were the last person she was thinking of when she was in another man's arms. You just weren't even in the equation Hemingway, sorry."

"No, I know. You're right, but it still kills me."
"It had everything to do with her, kid, not you. It was her heart, her love, and her feelings that turned to stone and sometimes good people lose battles son. You know how many good men died on those battlefields - men that should have never lost their lives to that shit.

"I can only imagine, Tex."
"Real life isn't like in Hollywood or massage parlors. They ain't all happy endings. We have been programed to believe

that the good guy will always win, horse shit. Bad guys win too.I mean, half the time I root for the bad guy on TV. Life is never fair; it's your job to make it as fair as possible."

"Think of a fight between a lion and a lamb," Tex continued after a pause.
"What?"
"A lion and a lamb. That lamb doesn't want to fight a lion, but it has no choice in the matter. The lamb will do everything in its power to survive. It will give its heart and soul but the lion will always win. Sometimes, life is a lion, kid, and you're the lamb. The goal is to never stop fighting when that lion attacks. This isn't the lion that's going to kill you, Hemingway. You're a tough fucking kid, remember that."

Again, Tex was the lighthouse in a storm. He was the calming whisper in a child's ear - like a gentle kiss on the forehead. He didn't need a degree from Yale or some alphabet soup doctorate degree after his name, charging an ever increasing co-pay in an uncomfortable waiting room. No, Tex had wisdom and an unparalleled understanding of the human psyche. He'd had his share of triumphs and disasters, and unlike most people, he'd taken those omens, those tricksters, those thieves of faith, and used them as learning tools.

"What is a triumph anyway? What's a disaster?" he asked, seeming to read my mind.
"Umm, I guess, it's . . ." Tex jumped in, "I'll tell you what they are; they are emotions, feelings, that's all. They are nothing

more than impostors. All they do is supply a false sense of oneself, either an accomplished or a self destructive one. And don't believe either." he admonished strongly, standing up and thanking me for the coffee. He turned towards his cabin mumbling, "I got shit to do today."

That following Thursday, a female coworker that I had admired from afar for as long as I could remember, approached me and started making small talk in the break room. I had always wanted to ask her on a date but my kitten balls had prohibited me from initiating such a move. As the gods of fate would have it, however, we reached for the same disposable coffee cup for our much-needed afternoon caffeine fix that work provided for free. I quickly conceded, removing my hand from the cup, apologized and stepped back. My coworker immediately recognized these as the gestures of a gentleman. She took the first upside down cup from the pile and stepped back to allow me to remove the next. We made eye contact while I said "screw it" to myself. I could hear Tex in my soul as if he was standing next to me. "The answer is always no, kid, if you don't ask the question."

"Hello, I'm Hemingway, James Hemingway. Sorry for trying to steal your cup."

"That's quite alright, I won't report you to H.R., she chided. "Hemingway you said?"

"Yes ma'am"

"Are you related to the author?"
"Third cousin on my mother's side. I used to go fishing with him all the time as a kid."

"That's incredible! I'm so jealous."
"Nah, just kidding. I couldn't catch a cold, let alone a fish."
"You're a funny one, Hemingway."
"What are you doing this weekend, anything good?" I asked.
"No, I tried to get tickets to the country festival but it sold out in less than ten minutes, so no, I'll be staying home like a good girl, maybe hit a yoga class and hang with my cat."

"I love cats", Hemingway said.
"Really, I do too. I love my cat!"
"I love them too, just with BBQ sauce."
"Your terrible, that's so mean."
"I know. It's an inside joke, but I actually have an extra ticket to the country fest if you're interested. My friend backed out and I was going to try to sell them online."

This was a total Santa Claus lie since not only didn't I have them, but I had absolutely no idea where to begin searching for tickets to the most popular concert of the season. As I was hoping she would say no, she exclaimed, "Yes!" We exchanged numbers quickly and as discreetly as possible and went back to our respective cubicles, hers donned with a picture of her cat, Lemon drop, mine with a picture of my daughters and favorite poem "If" by Kipling.

Panicked, I began to curse myself. "Welcome to the shit show, Hemingway, you did it again." However, one of the perks to living in the smallest state in the union is the simple fact that everyone knows someone, and that someone always has a friend who knows a friend. Whether it's a state job for your kid, reservations for a restaurant, or a snow removal contact for some obscure city parking lot, but in this case, it was for tickets to a sold out concert that was happening in less than seventy-two hours. Maybe that's the reason that there are more politicians in prison than in the State house? After a few phone calls and paying more than five times the face value amount, I was in possession of third row seats to the hottest show in town.

I called to make plans and coordinate the food and drinks for tailgating. She was just as excited to go to the show as I was at the prospect of having guilt free sex with the best looking girl in the office. She informed me that she had bought a new cowgirl hat for the occasion; that tidbit of information did not disappoint me in the least. At no point in my life could I recall seeing a female in a cowgirl hat and not think she was sexy. The fact that a cowgirl hat made an average woman look a hundred times better did not escape me. I wasn't going to ponder the phenomena but just accepted it as fact: Jane looked amazing in business attire, never mind a cowgirl hat! I would be the envy of all men at the office if they could see her in that hat and hopefully a pair of cut off jean shorts.

Prior to picking Jane up at noon time for the seven o'clock concert, I stopped and purchased the prerequisite items needed for a tailgating survival kit: a sleeve of red solo cups to throw off the scent for the recently hired bike patrol officers, pizza strips, prepackaged shrimp cocktail complete with cocktail sauce in the middle, a twelve pack of each of our favorite beer and a bottle of Tequila for when shit gets real. Oh yeah, I almost forgot, one roll of toilet paper for her; I ran back in.

I arrived at her condo at three minutes past twelve and Jane did not disappoint. She came out as soon as my car came into view. Her attire consisted of a pair of cowgirl boots, cut off jean shorts, a Lenard Skyward shirt that ended right below her belly button and a straw cowgirl hat. In her hands she carried a tray of home made cookies and a bottle of rum that she had bought when she was on vacation in the islands. By the look on her face, and the expeditious speed at which she walked to the car, I knew she really anticipated enjoying the day. She placed the cookies and bottle of rum on top of the car, with a blatant disregard for the decades old paint and opened the door. She put the items in first, followed by herself, then leaned over and fervently planted a kiss on my cheek while holding her hat so it wouldn't fall off of her head. She re-situated herself, grabbed the seatbelt and placed it perfectly between her surgically enhanced breasts.

"Thank you, Ralph Nader," I whispered.
"Who's that?"
"Oh, no one," as I smiled and put the car into drive.

Jane took charge of the dial that controls the radio stations like any well trained co-pilot does, and found the local country channel that was airing live from the concert's expansive parking area. A few minutes into the drive, she asked me to pull over into the next parking lot. At the same time Jane unbuckled the perfectly placed seat belt, she reached into the back seat to retrieve the bottle of rum. I did as I was told and pulled into the next convenience store. Jane jumped out of the car and ran in, never asking me if I wanted anything. Minutes later she appeared with a Big Gulp of diet soda. She sat back in the car and dumped out about three inches worth of liquid, opened the bottle of rum and replaced the void that she'd created. After a few clockwise stirs with the eighteen-inch straw that accompanied the monstrosity of a beverage, Jane gave me the first sip.

It was now twenty-three minutes past noon and we were already well on our way towards a hangover that would likely require as much time to recover from as minor surgery. The ride lasted about thirty minutes, just enough time for me to ascertain that Jane was a completely different person when she wasn't shackled by pant suits, dead lines, and cubicles.

We pulled into the parking lot along with all the other vehicles, which ranged from monster trucks to electric cars, several with pirate flags at full mast. Joe Security, complete with a short-sleeved shirt and black leather fingerless gloves, directed us to the parking spot that we would occupy for the next several hours. We exited the car and began to unload the chairs and survival kit. To an astute observer, the speed with which we operated was very impressive. This was obviously neither Jane's nor my first tailgate. She set up the two beach chairs while I placed the cooler in between. The venue held twenty-four thousand people, so it was safe to assume that twenty-three thousand; nine hundred and ninety-eight people had the same exact plans as we did. The entire parking lot was impregnated with colorful shirts, skirts, flags and coconut shell bikini tops, with the occasional straw hula skirt worn by a drunk, over weight man. There were people throwing footballs and grilling every food imaginable. In the background, we could hear six different radios playing six different songs, but somehow it all came together as a cohesive unit.

As soon as we sat in the beach chairs, mine with blue stripes, Jane's with pink, I opened the cooler and retrieved our respective beers, popped the tops and made a toast.

"May misfortune follow you your whole life, but never catch up."
"Perfect." Jane replied with a smile and bedroom eyes.
After a few beers and some shrimp cocktail, we decided to go for a walk and observe the craziness all around. Jane poured a beer into a red plastic cup for each of us before we set off down the row of cars. After a short walk we came upon a pick up truck with a professional DJ stand in the rear bed playing music. A crowd of people dancing around surrounded it. The DJ was offering a free CD to any woman who flashed her breasts, and just as I was about to utter "What tramp

would . . ." Jane ran towards the rear of the truck and lifted her shirt for the group of random men to observe. I was stunned but more importantly I was disappointed. I wasn't able to grasp the concept that a woman would show her breasts to strange men in exchange for a compilation of some insignificant person's selection of music. Oddly enough, I didn't know if I was more upset at the fact that I liked this girl, or that a group of jack-offs got to see her tits before I did. "Shit, if I known this was her M.O., I would have given her a CD months ago," I thought to myself.

I quickly came to one of two choices: 1) tell Jane exactly what I thought of her flashing random men - that I found it repulsive that she'd trade her dignity for a free CD, or 2) not say a word, and just recognize the date for what it was - good music, good beer and a potential sexcapade. Her actions just assured her a position as an insignificant spoke in the wheel of my life and that was feeling increasingly fine with me. After Jane flirtatiously spoke with Mr. Tits McGilicuddy for longer than I appreciated, she walked over holding the CD. I decided to ignore the transgression as we continued on our journey. Eventually we returned to our own parking lot oasis, ate some cold pizza and enjoyed a few more beers. The conversation was perfectly shallow, with no topic requiring even a cursory reading of the Wall Street Journal or one another's diary. We shared light work stories and amusing happenings from previous concerts.

The concert exceeded my expectations. The groups sounded better live - or maybe it was the energy that permeated the air. I wasn't a student of quantum physics but absolutely believed in the theory that Dark energy fills the emptiness in a room. I never tried to deny myself the feelings of energy, positive or negative, and thought people were ignorant who did. Just like a ship that sets sail from the harbor and slowly disappears from view, the ship still exists; you just can't see it anymore. Same as energy, I always said to my children. Just because you can't see it, doesn't mean it's not there.

I whispered loudly in Jane's ear, "Are you ready? I kind of want to beat the crowd to the cars, plus I'm not loving this song."

"I was thinking the same thing," Jane said.
"I guess those twelve dollar draft beers are kicking in" I jokingly added, making light of the fact that I was paying an obnoxious price for cheap, draft beer. My plan worked perfectly; we reached our car just as the concert ended and the sea of drunkenness flooded towards the parking lot. Out of respectful routine, I opened the passenger door for Jane. No matter what shit storm surrounded my life, I was always a consummate gentleman; chivalry defeated my depression on any given day. I sat in the car but before I could turn over the ignition, Jane leaned over and kissed me.

After the kiss Jane sarcastically commented, "I guess I had to make the first move!"

"Sorry, I obviously wanted to kiss you the second I saw you, but I didn't want to be disrespectful."

"Oh Hemingway, your so sweet. Thank you for such a wonderful day."

"No, thank you Jane; it was an honor to have you by my side today."

At that, she completely blushed and leaned over and kissed me again. While we continued to kiss passionately, I had an internal discussion on whether or not I should try to touch one of the breasts that Jane had exposed to the masses. The gentleman in me lost that battle and I began to slowly traverse up her shirt. Jane didn't flinch at all; on the contrary it turned her on. Her hands quickly moved to the crotch of my jeans that were growing tighter by the second. I completely disregarded the fact that we were still sitting in a parking lot surrounded by a sea of moving people, until a shirtless man knocked on the window and gave the standard sign of approval by placing his tongue between his two open fingers, while his three shirtless friends made horn signs.

"Shit! Let's get out of here," I said as I disengaged from the sex stupor that had hypnotized me. I carefully backed out of the parking space and made it to the main isle, where several cars were waiting to exit.

"I wish I was driving a monster truck right about now," I said to Jane as we were both looking at the endless row of illuminated break lights in front of us, most likely caused by the pressure of a flip flopped foot.

"A helicopter would be nice too," she replied.

"Next time, sorry."

The kissing continued when Jane spontaneously unzipped my fly. She then extracted my blood filled penis from its hibernation and stroked it several times until I was completely aroused. Leaning over, she put my erect penis in her mouth, completely stunning me. "Holy shit, I was content with just a kiss!" What better way to pass the time in a god-forsaken traffic jam than by getting a guilt free blow job from the hottest girl in the office, I said to myself. While Jane was perfecting her craft, I tried to concentrate on not having any involuntary leg movements, so we wouldn't rear end the pick up in front of us. I placed my head back on the headrest and enjoyed the sensation. I tried to put my hand up the leg of her jean shorts, or lack there of, but she gently guided it away. Jane wanted to focus and didn't want any distractions. As soon as we'd made it out of the traffic jammed parking lot and merged onto the highway, I was able to enjoy Jane's performance even more, now that it was less likely that some shirtless asshole would knock on the window and take a selfie with my penis in the background. The highway was a completely different story. Except for one obscure truck driver who hadn't had a decent meal in years, slowing down to watch the show, no one else was none the wiser, plus the voyeur in all of us gets turned on to the fact that some random person might catch you. I wasn't talking about having sex in the middle of a funeral procession, but the possibility of a hard working American driving a truck for eighteen hours a day seeing me getting a blowjob didn't bother me.

My wife, ex-wife that is, would never perform oral sex while I was driving, for the simple fact that I wasn't able to reciprocate. Everything was tit for tat in that marriage and sex was no exception. I told Tex once that I hadn't thought it was possible for someone to ruin a perfectly good blow-job, but she had succeeded. Numerous studies have shown that driving on the highway for a prolonged period of time can hypnotize you. I wondered if a study was ever conducted on oral sex and driving at sixty-five miles an hour. It must be a deathtrap, I thought, a deathtrap totally worth the risk though. After Jane had successfully removed the sperm from my penis, she sat up and spit out the seeds of life into the remnants of a rum and diet coke. What a terrible way to go; there could have been a doctor, a lawyer, or a teacher in that batch, each potential superstar now drowned in a sea of leftover watered down, warm, rum in a cup. It was such an injustice for those poor little bastards. I guess when my mother told me that I was one in a million, she was right. Jane was such a polite girl; she even apologized for not swallowing. What a polar opposite of my ex, who would yell at me if I came on her stomach, lecturing me if my sperm went inside her belly button. I, in contrast, had deemed the belly button as a perfectly located catch basin. I was realizing just how awful the past several years of my sex life had been, now that I was finally able to enjoy an ejaculation without worrying about the location of its landing. The rest of the drive home was pleasant; she was a very down to earth girl with the all around coolness of a modern day hippie without all the political ideology and armpit hair. For a split second, I'd wondered if maybe she was a transvestite; was that why she hadn't let my hand near her vagina? No, you're an idiot, I thought. I quickly refocused my brain and continued the conversation.

The idle chit chat lasted for a few minutes in her driveway before Jane leaned over and gave me a dry peck on the cheek, a gesture I greatly appreciated since less than ten minutes prior she'd had a million of my sperm swimming around in her mouth. Although she had drunk a half a bottle of Poland Springs, and was now chewing on a piece of spearmint gum, one could never be too sure.

CHAPTER 8

Perspectives and Priorities

As I PULLED into the uneven dirt drive littered with stone, I noticed two vehicles parked in front of the cabin next to mine. One was a white convertible, the other a black SUV. I surmised that one belonged to a woman, the other a man. No doubt an affair – a blatantly forbidden sexual encounter conducted in Depeche mode. No glorious story, just a couple of horny, middle aged, unhappy people wanting to screw each other while their spouses were most likely at home watching the kids and folding laundry. I didn't give it another thought and went to bed. As I lay there, I began to think of my ex- wife, however. I wondered if she had ever met at a place like this to soil our union, along with her under garments. Getting increasingly annoyed and still half drunk, I grabbed a pen off of Chico's table, carefully opened my haunted door and belly crawled over to the rear of the black SUV. I bent down and unscrewed the little plastic cap protecting the inflation valve of the rear passenger tire, then stuck the pen in to move the metal piece to the side and began to let the air out. This maneuver was much louder and time-consuming than I'd expected it to be. As I replaced the little cap and moved on to the next tire, I realized how immature I was behaving. I quickly low crawled back to cabin number three and fell asleep, only to be awoken about an hour later due to a man yelling "Fuck!" I just smiled to myself all snug in my bed. "Mission accomplished, asshole," I whispered out loud.

I recalled an old saying as I watched the early morning sunshine penetrate the cheap curtains that were failing at their job : "There's a fine line between a night of debauchery and a Sunday morning" - a line I'd crossed countless times as a youth, but not as of late. I reluctantly placed my feet onto the waxed hardwood floor, loaded eight scoops of coffee grounds into the maker, walked the three feet into the bathroom and proceeded to relieve myself for what seemed like an eternity. "Might have to build an ark" I said, trying to amuse myself. The coffee was finished brewing at about the same time I finished my morning urination. I poured the elixir into my favorite mug, purchased from the Salvation Army, entirely fitting since coffee had become my salvation. I put on a Louis Armstrong album and walked out onto the porch. "Ahhh . . . nothing like the feel of artificial carpet and some fresh air to start ones day." As I sat down in the wooden chair, having enjoyed my first mouthful of strong java, I couldn't help but think that there was something truly medicinal in the little things in life - a cup of good coffee, a great song, the sun shining on one's face, a hug from a child, the sight of a heart shaped leaf falling from a tree . . . No matter how seemingly small is a gift from the universe, it's value is potentially priceless. I'm now beginning to understand that stopping to notice such gifts is life's little escape hatch. Coffee and song were mine this morning.

Having returned to the cabin to refill my "Sexy senior citizen" cup, I turned around to walk back out and noticed Tex sitting on the only chair on the porch. I filled another cup, grabbed the matching chair from Chico's table and joined him.

"No Elvis this morning?" were his first words.
"Nope, not today old man. I'm hung over and needed a little Sachamo."
The next words that came out of Tex's mouth surprised me.
"It's a shame that he's only known for that one song; he's so much more than that. One of my favorite songs is "La Vie En Rose.""

"Holy shit, me too! What are the odds of that? I didn't think anyone else knew that one," I added.

"I'm what they refer to as a boulevardier," Tex said in a phony sophisticated voice, grossly exaggerating the word.

"Yeah right," I quipped, "and I have a trust fund."
"How was the concert?" Tex asked, changing the subject.
"Great, you would have been proud of your little buddy."
I informed him about the day's events, including the improper burial of all those lost souls in a disposable cup full of soda and rum.

Tex signified his approval by a head nod.

"You better not fall for that girl, though."

"Why not?"

"Because kid, any girl worth her weight in salt wouldn't have put your little package in her mouth on a first date, that's why. Do you think your special? She would have most likely gone down on anyone that brought her to that concert. It just happened to be you."

"Well, it's not that little, and I would like to think that I had something to do with it . . . the good conversation, my behavior as a good person . . . "

"Keep telling yourself that shrimp dick."

Once again Tex was probably right, I realized. "Thanks for killing my confidence you old bastard."

"Look, I'm not saying you aren't a great guy. I'm sure you were great to her, but just take it as a fun date. Don't try to build something on it, that's all I'm saying. She's not the one, and as far as I can tell, you're looking for the one. Am I right in thinking that?"

"Yes Tex, you're right, you're always right." I said with just enough sarcasm that Tex got the message that I would heed the warning without requiring a lecture on the topic, at least right now. The music stopped, so I rose from my uncomfortable but solid chair and turned over the album.

"That's the only shitty thing about listening to a record player I called out to Tex."

"What's that?" Tex yelled back through the screen door. "You only get a few songs worth of music, then you have to get up and flip it over - not like music today where there are playlists that go on for hours."

"No soul in that shit though; music today is as fake as a set of titties in a strip joint," Tex countered.

"True," I conceded, rejoining him on the miniature golf carpet, hearing the clicks and pops of the old record.

My brief exit had given Tex enough time to change topics. He began to talk about the burden that had been placed on him as a result of taxation.

"Do they forget that we had a revolution because of taxation years ago? It's all by design so a few can rule the country, Republicans and Democrats alike. The founding fathers were great men and rebels but don't forget who and what they were. They were all very wealthy lawyers and merchants, all aristocrats. Show me one farmer in that group and I'll show you a lie. This government was built by the rich, for the rich. Ahhhhh, they're just sucking the life out of me. I'm rambling on . . . I'll shut up now." Tex said to himself out loud.

"Enough about me, how are you doing?
"I'm surviving, I guess," I replied with no energy
"That's all you can do."
"I know, it's just that I had to cash out my only retirement
fund to give my ex half. Every penny of that fund came out
of my paycheck but I still had to give half to her, not bad for
someone screwing around on her husband. I had about a hundred grand in there and it was still growing, not by a lot, but
that was what I was going to live on when I retired, now I will
never be able to retire.

"Retire? What is that anyway? Retirement. Give me a break.
Retirement is as man made as that plastic cup your friend spit
into yesterday. Why do we humans think we are entitled to
retire? Could a farmer retire a hundred years ago? No. If he
did, his crops would dry up, and his family would starve. Now,
all of a sudden we all need to retire after a few years of work.
Life is about hard work, hard work until the day you die. Could
someone retire from hunting and gathering a thousand years
ago? Friggin retirement, give me a break, kid."

"Sorry Tex, I . . . guess."

"Look, I'd love for everyone to be able to retire when they
grow old - and enjoy the golden years of life, but that's not
how it's supposed to be. You work, you die, that's life. Where
do we get off on thinking we can do nothing for the last
twenty or thirty years of our lives? Do you know what retirement is?"

"No, but I'm sure you're about to tell me."
"Retirement is every weekend that you have taken off since the day you started working. You get to enjoy your retirement, only it's for two days at a time, broken up over the course of your life. And be happy if you have the opportunity to do that."

"Never looked at it that way," I mumbled. Again, I felt that Tex's logic made sense, but I certainly wasn't alone in my presumptions.

"We are all spoiled brats who think we deserve a toy, and then cry when we can't get it. Life isn't your friend; it's here to test you. It's here to break you. It's *your* job not to be broken. It's your job to find the omens and listen to the universe. It gives you advice on how to survive, but will you listen? I sure as hell do."
"You want to know the funny thing about money? Tex continued.
"Sure."
"Most people that have it, don't deserve it, and most people that deserve it, don't have it."
As profound a statement as that was, Tex followed it up by asking, "How was the blow job anyway?"

"Fine", I said, still pondering Tex's money theory. "I mean, is there such a thing as a bad blow job? It's like eating a slice of pizza at three in the morning when you're hammered; it could never be worse than good!"

Tex laughed at the comparison.

"I'm proud of you Hemingway. Tex never called me by my first name.

"I mean that. At least you're out there facing the world instead of curling up into the fetal position like you've been doing."

"Thanks Tex."

"It takes a strong man to stand up after being knocked down. You always hear people saying that life isn't fair. Well, nowhere does it say that it's supposed to be. Again, it's our perverted sense of entitlement. You fight life by getting out of bed every morning, even though every ounce of your being wants to pull the covers over your head. You fight by paying your bills on time, by offering a smile when the situation doesn't call for one. You fight by being a good man in a corrupt world. Life wants to beat the shit out of you, don't let it."

"I won't Tex, but it sure has been easier knowing that you're in my corner."

"You're not alone kid, don't ever forget that. There are a few ways how life tests you, the first being how you act when no one is watching – which shows your character. Next is how you treat people when they can't do anything for you, and the last is how you act under duress – not losing your head or your cool. You follow those rules and you'll always be the good guy in the fight. Always be a pedigree amongst mutts," he summarized.

"You are a good man Tex. I don't know what I would have done if you hadn't come into my life. You have no clue how dark the thoughts were that kept creeping into my head a few months back."

"Trust me kid, I do."

They spoke of suicide. Although neither mentioned the word, each knew exactly what the other meant. "I thank God that he didn't provide me the constitution needed to complete that act," I said, half ashamed of even admitting to having had those types of thoughts.

"Everyone has their demons kid; only some acknowledge them."
"I remember the day that I drove into this lot feeling like my life couldn't get any worse. I could sense my ex laughing at my predicament. When I begged her not to ruin me financially, I'll never forget that she told me to move into my parents' basement. I felt like such a chump, but now I know it was destiny. It was a kiss from the universe that brought me here. This wasn't a coincidence. This wasn't by happenstance. I drove into this lot by design. Whose design remains to be seen, but it was definitely meant to be."

"You got it kid, of course it was meant to be. You listened to the omens that the universe provided. It gave you a kiss, because it loves all. We are all nothing but energy. It was your boulevard of life to pull into this dirt drive. There are no coincidences; it was the higher power reminding you that he or she is present. Every person on the face of this ball of dust floating though one of millions of galaxies has experienced coincidences, from a simple sheep herder in some foreign land to the Pope. Everyone has had one or more unexplainable events happen during life. It's up to the person to accept it as a sign; if they don't, shame on them. I choose to listen to the universe Hemingway, and I think you're starting to as well. The soul of the universe attracts people together like magnets. I don't think for one second that winged angels fly around with bows and arrows. The angels I believe in are here among us. Maybe I'm one guiding you though your situation. When a passerby cuts a seatbelt and frees a trapped person in an overturned truck, maybe he was an angel that day. When a soldier dives on a grenade to save his friends - those are my angels."

"So do you think everyone is an angel?"
"Maybe, maybe not. Maybe angels happen when you need them."
"Do you think so, Tex?"
"I'm not saying I'm right. I'm just telling you that's what I believe, and it makes living a little more palatable. . . Just as I started to digest the powerful statements that had just been spoken, Tex ever so bluntly informed me, "I have to take a shit. God damn coffee goes though me like a bullet," Tex mumbled, as he walked away.

"One last thing," Hemingway called to Tex.
"What's that, kid?"
"Do you think she laughs at my car now when she drives past here?"

"Fuck her, if she does," Tex bluntly replied. "Don't ever allow your self worth to depend on the respect and thoughts of others, ever."

As I watched Tex walk towards his cabin, I couldn't believe that this hardened shell of a man, that had lived a life punctuated with the tragedies of war and hardships, believed in energy and angels live among us. As I tossed out the remainder of my coffee on the lawn, I checked my watch and realized that I only had thirty minutes to pick up my kids to take them for a bite to eat. I squeezed into the coffin-sized shower that had water pressure as strong as the spine of a politician, a shower so small it prohibited me from masturbating. (I had tried more than once and hit my elbow so many times on the side of the test tube like vessel that I thought I had caused a deep tissue bruise.) I continued to ponder what Tex had just told me, and came to the conclusion that quite possibly I in fact had been an angel that day years back, when I had talked a homeless woman off a bridge on my way home from work.

As I pulled into the driveway of the house on which I'd spent each year's tax return to maintain, the same house in front of which I'd hung the bird feeder on the yard's only oak tree, because as my youngest put it, "The birds are hungry daddy; we have to feed them." As with most fathers, my powers were useless against my loving five-year-old eyes looking up at me, full of heart-felt concern for the birds.

Did she change the mattress? Or was the same mattress on which we'd made love countless times still there? Was the kitchen table still there, the table where I'd made my family breakfast on the weekends? Does her new boyfriend sit in my imaginary assigned seat or is there a new seating chart? Is he at the head of the table? Does he know that the broken leg on the table was a direct result of my wife's pantyless body weight being thrust against it, pushing it across the room one drunken night? I remembered joking the next morning that the table must not have been union made in America. The flashback came to an abrupt end when I saw my children walk down the drive. As my girls entered the car, but before they buckled themselves in, I received far too many kisses to count – *that* is what life is now all about. Somehow God designed the human brain to release healing powers during your child's hug. I didn't have to understand the science behind it to know that it existed.

"Where do you want to go for lunchie?" I put an "ie" on most nouns and verbs when addressing my girls.

"Pizza, pizza!" they yelled in unison.
"Sounds good to me. Let's go!"
    I drove the extra twenty miles so we could enjoy our favorite pizza, one that a food critic from a national publication had recently named as one of the top ten pizza joints in the country. This was a rating I knew it deserved some twenty years prior to the article being published. It was a place where a pizza was still a pizza, and where the chef had never heard of Arugula, where a pool of grease rested inside each curled up piece of pepperoni, and the sixty year

old waitress acted like you were bothering her when you dared to place an order. It's where you sat at the same tables you sat in when your parents brought you there as a child. As the waitress, currently doubling as a hostess, told us to follow her, the girls were playfully arguing over who was going to get to sit on the same side as me. This was the only argument that I actually loved to hear. When we reached the table, the decision had been made by the little one. All three of us would sit on the same side, with me in the middle. When I looked up from the solid white, flip side of my paper placemat on which I was attempting to draw a mermaid, I looked around the dining room and noticed what I'd always noticed, but had never actually noticed. Parents were not being parents when their children were being children, adults who had surrendered to the mundane nature of their cookie cutter lives. Their magic was gone - the very same magic that is inside every child's heart. The adults were mindless drones on their cellphones, checking the insignificant status of distant friends whom they would most likely avoid if actually seen. I despised the habit people had of taking pictures of their food and posting them online. "Just eat the god damn thing! Do you think your false friends care what you're eating?" I would often rant to myself, or Tex if he was across the cooler, which doubled as my outdoor coffee table and fridge.

I deemed it far more important to focus on your children sitting across from you, than sending a college acquaintance from twenty years ago a picture of your salad and perfectly placed margarita in the background.

"When can we stay at your place daddy?"
"Yeah daddy, I really want to see it"
"Not now, honey bunny. I'm still trying to get situated, but soon, I promise." I lied to my kids, a lie I referred to as a Santa Clause lie. When your children are little, you lie to them to keep the sparkle in their eyes. You lie to them about the existence of a jolly, heavy set, bearded fellow flying around in a sleigh, delivering gifts to children all over the world. It's a lie for the greater good of their well being." So 'Santa Clause' had to lie to them about staying at the cabins. In reality, I was still embarrassed to call cabin number three my home. Thankfully, my parents lived a few minutes down the road and my bedroom remained the same as when I'd lived there as a child - same wallpaper and even the same shoe boxes full of baseball cards in the closet. So, when it came time for visitation, we would all stay at my parents'. The cabin, as a direct reflection of my life at this juncture - unstable, crumbling, and in major need of an overhaul, wasn't something I was ready to expose my beautiful girls to just yet.

I couldn't help but notice how nice the lawn looked when I dropped my girls off, "Son of a bitch, what is he, a greenskeeper at Fenway!" I thought. I could never figure out the perfect mixture for the lawn - too much lime one year, not enough fertilizer the next; no matter what the the arithmetic was, it was always wrong. Not for the lack of trying though. I always gave a valiant effort to keep a perfectly manicured lot, but it wasn't in the cards. The girls reluctantly exited the car with watery eyes and heavy hearts as I shook my head every so slightly in acknowledgement of such a shitty situation. The drive home was filled with memories of the conversation we'd just had at dinner.

"If only snow had sugar, Daddy, it would be awesome!" my little one had exclaimed.

That magical piece of philosophy carried me all the way home without crying. When I arrived at the cabins, I dropped off the left over pizza and a spinach pie to Tex.

"Thanks kid, I love that place. There's no pineapple on this, is there?"
"No sir."
What's wrong? You okay?
"Yah, I'm fine," but before I could end that sentence with a "thanks", Tex interrupted me with the usual "Don't bullshit a bull-shitter."

"I miss my kids pal. I feel like a complete failure, only being allowed to take them for a few hours and having to drop them off right afterwards. If I'm one minute late in picking them up, she'll make up some excuse why I can't get them. God forbid I drop them off five minutes after the court order states; she'd file a police report for kidnapping and take me back to court. I feel so alone, so incomplete when they aren't with me pal, it just kills me, that's all."

"Me too kid; you're not alone. You're never alone. There are millions of people experiencing the same thing as you right now."

"Yeah, but they aren't in my head; they don't count."
"Well, I'm right here and I count."
"What do you mean?"
"I miss my son too. You'd be an asshole if you didn't miss yours. But at least you get to see them every other weekend. Some parents don't have that luxury. My only kid is lying in a field of stones on the Connecticut line."

"I'm so sorry Tex, I had no idea. I'm such an asshole for bitching about my situation."

"Nah, that's alright kid, you didn't know because I never told you."
"What happened? Do you want to talk about it?"
"Nah, nothing. It happened a long time ago," Tex said as he got up and walked into his cabin with the leftovers. "Thanks for the food," he yelled out as the screen door closed.

Deciding it was best not to knock on the door - to let Tex be - I walked back to cabin number three and called it a night. But this night was different. As I placed my head on the refreshingly cool pillow I had just turned over, I decided to pray. It was an unfamiliar gesture – not practiced since my days of taking chewable vitamins and attending Catholic school, so I just started talking to God about life. I asked for the protection of my family, somewhat reluctantly including my ex-wife. I asked God to shepherd me though the free will thinking that had taken me this far. I finished by asking God to cradle the loved ones that were not with us anymore, including Tex's child. There is great solace in praying I thought to myself, as a wave of love traversed though my soul. It was a love much larger than myself - a universal love of all things - an overarching assurance that 'Everything will be alright.' "Thank you" I said out loud.

CHAPTER 9

─── ⚜ ───

Stiffed Again . . .

As I WAS getting dressed for work that Monday, after my first interoffice hook up, I cringed at the thought of seeing Jane again. What do I say? How do I act? I avoided both the break room and the bathroom during the first few hours, but nature overpowered my desire of avoidance. I couldn't contain the urge any longer, plus I really wanted my afternoon cup of coffee. "You're being an idiot" I said to myself as I walked to the restroom and grabbed a much needed coffee. And as if fate was playing a cruel joke, Jane walked in moments after I did to retrieve a previously placed Tupperware container from the microwave. Much to my surprise, Jane acted as if nothing had occurred two days prior. Apparently she didn't want to tarnish her reputation at work, as much as I had changed my mind about wanting to date her. "Perfect." I thought. Small talk ensued and each of us quickly retreated to our respective cubicles, i.e., someone's perverted idea of the American dream.

Weeks went by with unvarying ways other than that the snow began to fall. The winter brought with it depression, and a sense of sadness that I had always felt watching the brown, lifeless leaves descend from the trees, exposing the fragile, charcoal grey limbs naked to the impending harshness of mother natures cruel joke. Together with the frail weeds reaching up to the heavens for God's help, they created a scene right out of Dante's Inferno. I hated braving the cold nights alone, feeling that a human being was designed to crave the warmth of a body, at least to hear the beating of your lover's heart lulling you to sleep. Whatever the recipe, I realized that I was missing the main ingredients. I assumed that the gray permeating the sky had started to have an affect on my ex as well, due to the fact that the frequency of harassment increased. My paycheck was garnished each week for child support, but she still found it necessary to ask me for half of the cost of ice skate sharpening. The fact that I purchased the girls expensive ice skates and name brand winter jackets had not resonated with my ex. She wanted that seven dollars from me, and she reminded me several times a day with texts that ended with numerous exclamation points. Didn't she know that it's grammatically incorrect to use more than one?

Once I told Tex about the recent barrage of texts and emails in regards to seven dollars, he chastised, "Why are you playing catch with her?"

"What?"
"Your playing catch with her, not with a ball, but with words. Stop playing catch. If you don't throw them back, she won't be able to catch them, and hurl them at you. And pay the seven dollars. Should you have to, no, it's ridiculous that she's

even asking for it, but for seven dollars you will purchase your sanity. She's trying to pick a fight with you so she can stay relevant in your life. No one wants to be forgotten, and you're starting to forget. She wants a reaction from you. She wants hatred from you, because that's an emotion; hate is the twin to love. They are the same - nothing but emotions that are birthed from the same place in your brain. Indifference, on the other hand, is power; once you're indifferent towards her, you have won the battle. All this back and forth, hatred, crying that you do - that's her controlling your power. Once you become indifferent, you take your power back and she will know. But only time will allow you to truly become indifferent; all the shrinks and drinks won't do it. Time brother, only time."

I took the advice and mailed a check to my old house for seven dollars and fifty cents - fifty cents! She actually included the fifty cents I muttered to myself while I waited in line to buy the stamp. I also took Tex's advice to only contact her in regards to the children and nothing else. She continued to hurl verbal pitches in my direction but I refused to catch. After a few weeks of practicing the new philosophy, the volume of texts dramatically decreased. The old man was right again.

The next Sunday brought with it a crisp cool morning breeze, that November always brings, but that didn't prevent Tex from knocking on cabin number three for his morning coffee and Elvis. I knew better than to complain about the weather and brought the other wooden chair out to the porch. I'd made that mistake once and Tex had told me about how he had almost froze to death in a foxhole wearing a thin, canvas jacket in sub-zero temperatures. I poured two black coffees and joined him outside. "Black like your soul," I said to Tex, handing him his coffee. After the first sip, I blew into my cupped hands to warm them up.

"Can you tell me what happened to your child?"

Tex inhaled deeply, not out of annoyance or frustration with the question posed, but to alleviate the pressure that formed inside his chest whenever he discussed the loss of his only child.

"I had a son. He was a great kid, my only one. He was driving home from his shift one night around seven thirty when a drunk ran a red light, and broad-sided him. He was killed on impact, but of course as cruel as life is, the prick that hit him walked away without a scratch, not even the inconvenience of a bloody nose or a black eye.

"Oh my God, I'm so sorry" I replied, almost whispering. "Thanks, It's been a long time but it never gets better. You just figure out a way to live your life a little easier, I guess. I'd even make the argument that it gets worse."

"What happened to the person that hit him?"
"Oh, you should have seen the trial, talk about a kangaroo court. He hired a team of highfalutin assholes to represent him. I was told they were all fellow country club members.

He got less time for killing my kid than some poor fucking black kid in the projects who steals baby formula to feed his kid. He was out in eighteen months, eighteen months for murdering my only child; can you believe that shit? I try not to think of it because it is enough to make me want me to do something I'd regret. So when you speak of injustice kid, trust me, I get it."

I just sat in complete silence not knowing what to say. Then Tex continued.

"I still remember the doctor telling me in the hospital that he's in a better place now.' Really? How would he know? He was in a perfect place with me, here on earth. I hate when people who have never experienced loss like that, say such things, like 'I know how difficult this must be.' My wife had to grab me because the doctor was about to be the recipient of my misplaced anger. Jesus, that woman was a saint; she was the only person who truly understood me and all my faults."

"The doctors probably just don't know what to say."

"I know, I was wrong, but trust me, there is nothing anyone can say or do at that moment to ease your pain. They just shouldn't say anything. It just pisses me off. I'm not saying I'm right; that's just how I feel. My wife passed away some years later. Well, her flesh and bone passed away ten years later but trust me, her soul died that day in the hospital. Her light went out, never to return. Her eyes never glimmered, and her smiles were never genuine after he died. Technically she died of cancer, but I know she had already died of a broken heart. So when you tell me that you only get to see your kids every other weekend, remember that there are parents out there that would walk the circumference of the earth to see their children for just *one* more weekend, but can't. Their voices and laughter can only be heard as a distant memory, the unique gait that each person possesses never be seen again, all those insignificant attributes that separate each one from everyone else – just gone, forever."

"I don't know if I could go on."

"Well, next time you hug your kids, remember that. Tell them how proud of them you are and how much you love them, because tomorrow is never promised. I didn't tell my son enough. I was hard on him because I wanted him to be strong in a tough world; I wanted him to be the best. I never sat with him and talked about life, or gave him advice and guidance. My role in his life was as a disciplinarian. I missed my chance. Don't miss yours Hemingway."

"I'm sure you were a great father Tex. He knew it then and he knows it now. You're a great man, and he was lucky to have you as a father."

"It's ironic how life works though. It took the loss of my child to see the errors of my ways. I'm such a better person now, but I will never have the opportunity to show him how I've changed. I wish I was the man I am now, when he was alive, but it's too late."

"Tex, I know you're always the one giving me advice. You have always been the rock, but now it's my turn. You're a good and honorable man, one that fought for his country when his country didn't fight for him. You never bitch and complain, even though your trials and tribulations have been significant. Maybe you were tough on your son, but that's how you knew to love him. Life is about forward progress, and your progress didn't stop at the death of your child. Most people would have given up, but you choose to continue the fight. You provided a home, structure, and love, plus you had married a good woman.

"A great woman" Tex interrupted. "Sorry, a great woman."

"But that's why he grew into a successful man; it was a direct result of you being a good man Tex, don't forget that. I am positive now that it wasn't some random event that I pulled into this lot that day. All the events in our lives were omens that brought us together. The universe sent me to you Tex, I truly believe that now; you're one of the angels you told me about."

"You're crazy kid, I'm no angel."

"Bullshit Tex. You told me yourself, that maybe you were, I have been thinking a lot, a lot about life. Our paths crossed for two reasons, the first one being was for you to save mine, just by your listening and allowing me to vent. All the advice you have given me, and just simply letting me know everything is going to be alright. The great advice you provide to me – it's the fatherly love you always had but didn't know how to express to your son, and how you have opened my eyes to the soul of the universe. I can't thank you enough, Tex. Honestly, I can't. The other reason I came here was to save you. You see your son in me. All the advice you provide - it's the fatherly love you didn't give him Tex, don't you see it? You're making up for not giving it to your son. Remember you told me about the lion and the lamb? Well, you've killed a shitload of Lions Tex."

"Maybe your right, kid." Tex said as he asked for something strong. The depth of the conversation clearly both wounded and healed him.

I went inside and grabbed an unopened bottle of twelve-year old whiskey I'd received as a Christmas gift the year before. After emptying the coffee from both mugs, I poured two fingers worth in each.
"I was saving this for a special occasion; I guess this is it," I commented upon my return.

"You know whats funny about special occasions?
"What's that?"
"You never know you were in one until it passed."

We sat in silence, digesting what had been said, and sipped our room temperature whiskey that wasn't diluted with ice cubes . The coldness that surrounded us was replaced by the heaviness of the moment and the warmth of the whiskey. I could feel it, and was quite sure that Tex could too. He finished his drink with one final gulp, stood up and shook my hand.

All he said was "Thanks kid." and that was enough. Even though I was in my early forties, I was still considered a kid to Tex. I just smiled in acceptance of his graciousness. I continued to sit on the lopsided porch, my coffee mug resting on the cooler for a little while longer. I started to see the ocean through the water. "This is part of my journey; this is all meant to be," I said to myself, finally feeling that my life was coming together. I stood up and tilted my head back to allow the last of the whiskey to traverse down my throat. "You'll be alright kid," I told myself again as I looked out into the bleakness of winter's imminent approach.

Later that day I was jolted by a loud banging on my front door, followed by a loud, familiar voice.

"Hemingway! Open up."

I opened the door as quickly as it took me to walk the four feet across the cabin. "What's up?" I then noticed Tex holding his left hand above his heart, wrapped in a blood soaked towel.

"Jesus! What happened?"

"Ah, I was cutting up some cardboard boxes and the razor slipped. It's not that bad."

It was that bad, but I knew that Tex was the kind of guy to downgrade everything significant, including an injury that required immediate medical attention.

"Sorry to bother you, but I can't shift with my hand the way it is. Can you drive me to the V.A.?"

"Yeah, of course. Let me grab my coat."

"Grab me a god damn beer while you're at it."

I did as I was told, and handed Tex a Miller High Life for the ride. When we walked into the emergency room, I was surprised to see people from so many different walks of life. Although I had no preconceived notions of who belonged in the VA, I hadn't expected to see a black woman – who was missing her arm - sitting next to an aging biker with a long gray beard who was wearing a faded jean jacket under a leather vest with more patches than I could count. Soldiers from different eras and wars, but their sacrifices were the same, and sacrifice knew no time and color. Tex checked in with the woman behind the sliding glass window and sat beside me under the picture tube television. As I was thumbing through the wrinkled pages of a magazine dated from the previous year for what seemed an eternity, but was actually just forty minutes, a nurse opened the door and called out.

"Walter Roy"

I didn't flinch, but Tex stood up and started to walk towards the nurse.

"Walter? Your name is Walter?" I said in astonishment.

"Yeah, why?"

"Nothing, I guess it fits, Walter, huh."

Tex continued towards the nurse with his hand elevated above his heart to reduce the throbbing.

"Does your son want to come in with you, Mr. Roy?"

Tex didn't correct her. "No, he can stay there."

After about an hour the nurse came out and asked me to follow her.

"The doctor would like to speak with you in regards to his out-care treatment."

"Sure"

I walked through the curtains and saw Tex sitting up on the bed with an annoyed look on his face, possibly because he had just been poked and prodded with needles, but more likely because his carelessness had caused this visit. The doctor turned around and looked at me. She was a very attractive blonde woman with piercing blue eyes. I soon realized that Tex had coordinated my entry into this room, so he could make an introduction.

"Doc, this is my neighbor, Hemingway. Could you please go over the medication I need for this nonsense?"

Yup, total set up, I thought to myself, as I remembered the only occasion I had offered Tex an aspirin, and he had replied with the exact words: "Those are for pussies."

In her Russian accent, the doctor began to explain the procedures to ensure an uninfected and successful recovery.

"Thank you Doctor Denisov," I said slowly as I read her name tag.
"My name is Natasha, and I trust that Walter will be well cared for?"
"I'll try my best. If not, I'll just have to put him down."
" Try it, Kid, you'll need an army." Tex interjected.
The beautiful, yet intimidating doctor handed me the papers for treatment, and a few prescriptions for drugs more addictive than heroin.

"Maybe you should put your number on there in case I have a question," I said, not believing that those words had just come out of my mouth.

Natasha smiled and looked at me, then at Tex.
"What do you think I should do? Do you think he needs my number?" she asked Tex.

"Nah, he's a smart kid, he can figure it out." Tex said with a shit-eating grin on his face. "That's for telling her, you'll put me out to pasture."

We all had a good laugh as the good doctor decided to write her cell phone number on the discharge paper. As we reached the truck, I opened the passenger door for Tex, a gesture he was not pleased with, which he made eminently clear: "I'm not dead yet, I can get my own God damn door."

"You're close enough pal."
"What are you trying to say?"
"Nothing, I just wouldn't buy any green bananas if I were you," I chided opening the driver's side door.

"You're welcome," Tex said unprovoked.
"Thanks pal, that was a very nice gesture, asking me to come in there to go over the paperwork. I knew what you were doing, and it is much appreciated, you sly old, fox, you."

"I still got it, kid."
As we pulled into the cottages I thanked Tex again.
"Thank me for what?"
"For cutting your hand."
"For cutting my hand?"
"Yeah, if you didn't cut your hand I would have never met Natasha, I guess you were right after all; everything happens for a reason."

"Not me slicing my hand, you bastard."
Nope, the universe doesn't discriminate Tex. You said it yourself, for every action, there is an equal or greater reaction."

Tex took a deep breath and conceded, "Your welcome Hemingway. Just put the keys above the visor."

The next week I played phone tag with Natasha, but my last three texts went unanswered. Just as I was about to give up, I received a reply.

"Sorry, been busy at work LOL.
Again with LOL! At no point in the conversation was a laugh out loud required – or even appropriate. LOL was the pebble in the shoe of text messaging, I decided.

Accepting that her schedule was not conducive to a productive social life, and in hopes of seeing her naked, I disregarded the sophomoric LOL, and replied. Our playful texting eventually lead to a date that Saturday night. I didn't care for that form of communication, for the simple fact that so much was lost in translation. Why was the text so short? Was it a sign of disinterest or simply that the person was busy? At least there weren't an over abundance of grammatically incorrect exclamation points, I conceded.

We made plans to meet at an upscale sushi restaurant in town. I wasn't entirely pleased due to the fact that you usually leave those places more hungry than when you arrived. I was also well aware that this could be another hundred dollar meet and greet. Upon arriving, I admired the fact that the walls were painted with heavy reds, and that a ten foot Buddha was the centerpiece in the middle of a koi pond. Not to mention that on the weekends they removed the tables at ten o'clock to make room for the dance floor.

I arrived a few minutes early and sat down at the bar. The bartender came right over and poured the cabernet I ordered. I sat alone and just enjoyed the taste and effect of the first sip of wine after a long week, resisting the urge to dilute the experience by web surfing on my phone or reading the subtitles on a news channel explaining its distorted version of current events. As I was day dreaming at how pleased George Washington would have been to drive a car during the Revolutionary War, instead of freezing on his horse while riding up and down the eastern seaboard, Natasha tapped me on the shoulder.

"Is this seat taken?"
"Not at all, how are you? I asked, while I stood up and gave her a light embrace.

"You look like you were in deep thought. What were you thinking about?"
"Nothing, you'll think I'm insane."
"Oh boy, now I'm curious. You have to tell me."
"Well, I was just thinking about my car. I was complaining to myself that it's old and in need of a few repairs. Then I thought how pleased George Washington would have been if he had been able to drive my car - with all it's heat and air conditioning - around the battle fields, instead of riding his horse. He would have loved it, so I was telling myself, if my

car is good enough for George Washington, then it's good enough for me."

"You're right, you are insane," she said with a big smile on her face. "I guess in some bizarre way, it makes sense though."

The waiter came over and inquired as to what she wanted to drink. "I'll have a vodka, neat, please."

"I guess stereotypes are earned," I commented, as we decided to remain at the bar for dinner.

"Dah, Dah." She answered.
"What kind of sushi do you like?"
"I like it all. Order whatever you want and we'll share," she replied.

I did like the *idea* of sushi. There was something intimate about the communist idea of sharing one another's food, plus it was a healthy alternative in case the night ended with my shirt coming off. At least I wouldn't be bloated from a burger and fries or eight ounces of pasta.

"So how do you know Walter?"

I had been dreading that question, because I'd been dreading admitting the answer. Even though I had accepted my own fate of living in a lopsided cabin with green Astroturf covering the front porch, I didn't go around telling people, let alone a perspective sexual partner. But as my college girl-friend had so eloquently phrased it when she dumped me, "It is what it is." So I told her the tale that had been my life for the past couple of years, both good and bad. "Well, that's my story, what's yours, doc?"

"Well, I was married twice; my second husband committed suicide last year."

"Oh, I'm so sorry, that must have been awful," I said as sympathetically as I could, not knowing the circumstances.

"No, it's nothing, but thanks though," she said as she reached for another piece of spicy tuna. Who reaches for spicy tuna, after talking about her husband's suicide? I wondered to myself.

"What about your first husband?"
"He passed away as well."
"He did?" I said as I almost fell off my barstool. "What happened?"
"He passed away in his sleep; the doctors think it was a heart attack."
"That's terrible. How old was he?
"Thirty seven"
"Thirty seven? Wow, that's young to die of a heart attack."
"I know," Natasha replied nonchalantly, as she flagged down the bartender for another vodka.

Holy shit, I thought to myself. Did she kill these two poor bastards or does she have the worst luck on the planet? And how the hell could I be contemplating having sex with this woman; she's a black widow! My internal dialogue lasted for a few minutes but luckily she was busy checking her emails on her work phone, and didn't notice the look on my face. How is my penis this much stronger than my brain? I mean, I'm a smart guy. Why am I not leaving? She could literally murder me tonight. She either killed her two husbands, or she drove one to suicide, and the other to have a heart attack. Either way it's not good. When Natasha was finished checking her phone, she turned and looked back at me.

"Did I scare you off?"
"Hell yes" I said to myself.
"Not at all," I lied out loud.

By the time our plates were cleared, the staff began to remove all the tables to make way for the dance floor. Besides the fact that she most likely murdered her last two husbands, I was starting to enjoy my date. We remained sitting at the bar while the lights were lowered and people started to migrate to the dance floor once the music began to play. The volume was just the excuse I was looking for to lean in closer to Natasha in order for each to hear the other. She informed me about the pitfalls of being a doctor, such as the lack of sleep and gym time. "Everyone thinks we are healthy because we know the science and statistics, but in actuality it's a very unhealthy, stressful lifestyle."

"You must be doing something right because you look great," I replied, in hopes that the Russian assassin would take pity on me if she were to take me home. After she finished her third vodka, she led me onto the dance floor. Although I was not particularly fond of the ritual, I went along and did exactly what my room mate in college told me do to when it came to dancing: "Listen my man, all you need to do is write the alphabet in the air with your ass, that's it."

The move had worked since September of ninety-two and I wasn't about to change it now. As I reached the letter W, Natasha kissed me. She kissed me just how I imagined that a Russian would kiss, machine gun strong, and lacking the romance of a French poet.

"Let's get out of here," she said.
"Ok, where to?" I asked, hoping she would say anywhere besides her place - for the sake of my longevity.

"My place."
"Sounds good."
I quickly paid the tab and tipped thirty percent just in case karma actually existed, and again, another date, another time stiffed I thought to myself. As I was following her back to the house I wondered what Tex would be saying about this. Would he be proud that I was trying to bed a pinko commie, or would he call me an idiot for attempting to have sex with a Russian assassin, who tops the short list of people who murdered her last two husbands? How would she do it? A gun? A knife? Would she bludgeon me with a lamp? Poison? Yes, that's what she'd use, poison, it's much less messy than

a antique, brass lamp to the back of my skull. Ok, now that I suspected what means she would use to try to kill me, I told myself: "Just don't drink anything when you're there and you'll be fine."

As we were standing on her front steps, she began to unlatch the three locks on her front door - the standard door-knob lock and two additional deadbolts.

"I guess no one is breaking in here, huh?" I commented.
"Or escaping," Natasha jokingly replied.

I had ascertained more than enough information to real-ize that I needed to leave, but suffered from the same syn-drome that most men do. I had named it "demon semen", because when the prospect of sexual intercourse neared, I lost all rational thought and only thought with my penis. A man could be intelligent enough to split the atom or make bil-lions in the stock market, but wasn't smart enough to walk away from a woman when he should. That was the root cause of why the human population went from zero to seven bil-lion people in a few thousand years - all because of "demon semen... and booze, booze helped too.".

Once we gained access, she relocked all three mechanisms.
"You took away my escape route," I said nervously.
"Sure did, want a drink?"
"Sounds good," I responded, taking less than ten seconds to break the potentially life-saving promise I'd just made to myself moments prior. As Natasha walked into the kitchen to

retrieve whatever liqueur she planned to use to mask the poison, I walked over to the mantel and noticed several black and white military pictures. One was a platoon standing at attention. Another was of a man sitting on the top of a tank with a rifle in his hands and a cigarette hanging out of the corner of his mouth, but it was the last picture of several men standing behind a table with a Nazi flag draped over the front that surprised me. Natasha came back with two glasses of a clear liquid, vodka I assumed. "What are these pictures?" I inquired.

"They are of my grandfather during World War II."
"Are you German?"
"Nein," she answered, "one hundred percent Russian."
"Then why is there a Nazi flag in this picture? If my memory serves me correctly, didn't the Germans invade Russia?

"True, but my grandfather hated Stalin and communism, so he joined some Russian Liberation Army; they fought with the Germans against Russia."

"Interesting"
"He loved Russia and wasn't interested in German world domination but he wanted to get Stalin out, so he and a few of his friends joined the movement."

"Interesting. Never heard of that before. What is this we're drinking?" I asked, holding up my glass and looking through it.

"It's vodka you can only get from Mother Russia," she answered in an exaggerated, perfect Russian accent. "I snuck it though customs last year."

"Must be smooth," I said.
"Dah, Dah," she replied, as she raised her glass and made a toast in Russian. She then translated it to English so I could understand.
"May we always have a reason to party."

We raised and touched glasses. I quickly, but reluctantly, took a mouthful.
"It's like water."
"Told you so," Natasha said.
    Much to my relief, I didn't feel lightheaded or dizzy after that first sip, so I decided to enjoy the rest of the contraband vodka without concern for my demise permeating in my head. Natasha looked at me with her piercing European eyes, and pushed me down on the couch. She placed her drink on top of the fireplace mantle that was now glowing red with fire from a fire starter log she'd bought at the super market. "Imagine," I'd said, as I lit the fire moments prior to being pushed onto the couch, "Starting fire hundreds of years ago required skill, and took people all day. Now, anyone with a lighter can create it, incredible."

"Shut up, Hemingway." Natasha was clearly not in the mood for my eccentric observations of life.

"Sorry" I said, as my ass hit the cushions on the couch. She remained standing in front of me. She had one hand behind my head, while the other was removing her tight black stretch yoga pants. There, she stood naked from the waist down in complete control of the situation. She thrust my head into her cleanly shaven crotch. Just as in my dance moves, I incorporated the same movement for oral sex; I wrote the alphabet with my tongue, instead of my ass. After all, it's nature chess match, I said on more than one occasion to my friends. I wondered if the women in my life knew that I wrote the letters of the alphabet on their vaginas? Apparently, it was working though, because it felt like she was about to rip my hair off the top of my head. She could barely stand after she orgasmed, completely satisfied, her knees buckled as she fell onto the couch next to me. I, being aroused, attempted to continue with my finger. I played with her vagina but she pushed my hand away. "It's much too sensitive Hemingway, sorry." Minutes passed by like hours as Natasha laid motionless next to me not saying a word. I felt my chest tighten as my penis softened. As the look of contentment on her face was illuminated by the flames, she said, "I had such a wonderful time this evening. You're an absolute gentleman, but I must be getting to bed. I have to be up in a few hours."

From the inflection in her voice, I knew that it was time for me to leave. As I stood up from the couch, I tried to amuse myself by noting that 'at least I don't have to get dressed.' I leaned over the still-naked-from-the-waist-down Natasha and kissed her forehead. "Good night honey, sleep tight."

With that, I showed myself to the door. Walking to the car, I began to laugh out loud at the situation. "At least she didn't kill me, I said." While driving home I couldn't help but think of the irony of the evening; I now knew how all those women felt after giving a blowjob and receiving nothing in return. I belong on the wall at the walk of shame hall of fame. Just then, as if the universe was smiling upon me, "Born in the USA" came on the radio. I quickly turned up the volume and sang along with the Boss while pumping my fist in the air.

CHAPTER 10

·⚜·

Magnets Aren't Always Metal

A STUBBORN KNOCK shattered the beautiful silence of an early morning. "What?" I yelled though it.

"Get your ass up!"

"I'm sleeping!"

"There's plenty of time to sleep, when you're dead!"

"Alright, alright, I'm coming. Hold your horses." I said as I performed a quick horizontal stretch.

"Hurry up, it's freezing out here, Tex grumbled, as he heard the door being unlocked. I opened the door in my boxer shorts to the disapproval of Tex, but before he could complain, I walked back and put on a pair of sweatpants.

"What time is it anyway?" I asked.

Tex stood red faced wearing a black knit sailors cap and Navy peacoat, informing me that it was "zero seven hundred hours." I could tell by the dry, red coloring of his skin with the watering of his blue eyes that he had been outside for a while. As I started to make the coffee I asked what Tex was doing outside at this hour.

"I was shoveling."

"Oh," I said, surprised at the revelation of snow on the ground. "I would have helped."

"Nah, keeps me young, plus, I don't want you getting hurt." Tex replied, as he twisted from side to side to alleviate the stiffness brought on by the lifting and frigid temperature. Tex sat at Chico's table and blew into his hands. As always, the coffee was perfect. It was probably the only aspect of my life that I hadn't screwed up I told Tex. I placed an unopened package of Stella Doro cookies on the table and sat on the edge of the bed. "I haven't had these in years."

"Neither have I, not since my wife passed away."
"She sounds like she was a good woman."
"The best." Tex put simply.
"You make a great cup of coffee, kid."
"Thanks." I knew that compliments weren't given often, so I needed to appreciate them when they came. Tex was tough on me most of the time. When I was depressed, he told me to toughen up. When I was excited, he would warn me not to let it lull me into complacency. But my coffee, that was never an issue with Tex. He loved it, just as much as he loved visiting, and having me in his life.

"Remember the doctor you set me up with?"
"Who, the cute, little commie?"
"That's the one. I took her out last night."
"Good for you, did you make your country proud?"
"Not even close."

"What happened?" Tex said as he dunked a cookie into his black coffee.

"Where do I begin? For starters, her last two husbands died before the ripe old age of forty, one by suicide, the other a heart attack. Then she made me perform oral sex on her, after which she immediately fell asleep, and pretty much kicked me out of her house. And oh yeah, her grandfather was a Nazi."

"Ha! That's great! Tex laughingly said. I bet those poor sons of bitches had life insurance policies."

"You really think she could do that?"
"Did you see those blue eyes? They were sexy as hell, but friggin' evil." So you didn't get laid?"
"Nope, it's complicated."
"Getting laid is always complicated, except at a whore house in Asia, then it's not complicated," Tex said, speaking from his experience being stationed overseas.

Tex found the story amusing but expressed his disappointment in the fact that I didn't conquer a Nazi's granddaughter.

"In hindsight, it's better that you didn't get laid last night though. Your life is a shit show right now, and the last thing you need is some scorned Russian commie sneaking over here poisoning our coffee or slicing your tires, speaking of which, you need to rotate yours."

"I know I do."

"I guess it makes sense - I could totally see that happening - but I just can't seem . . ."

Tex interrupted me - "Now before you start getting all sensitive on me, turn the record over." I resumed where I had left off after returning from putting on the B-side of Vaughn Monroe.

"I just can't find a good one Tex, I mean I've been on a handful of dates now and each one seems worse than the last. I got used for oral sex, yelled at over a fucking cat, and was blamed for the warming of the earth; I just can't catch a break."

"Don't give up kid."
"I won't, but it feels as if the world has grown since my divorce. It seems so much bigger now that I'm facing all it has to offer by myself. The nights are darker and the winter is colder. When you're with someone you love, all those insignificant things add up. I can't explain it. It's like a constant sorrow that I can't snap out of.

"You will kid. Life is meant to be shared. Look at your body; it has two of everything, two eyes, two ears, two legs, two arms, two nostrils. It's no coincidence that nature designed us to depend on duality. We need a partner for balance, not only physical balance, but mental and spiritual balance as well. Just stay the course and continue to find yourself, don't become stagnant. Everyday should show forward progress, either by learning, going to the gym, reading, or taking a class. Always be better than you were yesterday, remember that."

"Thanks Tex, I knew you would give me some type of pep talk."
"I'm not saying those things because I like hearing myself talk. You're a good kid Hemingway; your moral compass points true North. Each day, do your best. Depending on the day, your best will vary, but always follow your moral compass and the universe will reward you. Just make sure you listen to it. And remember, there are no coincidences, that I promise."

"You've said that before Tex, you really believe it, don't you?"
"I know I've said it before, because it needs to sink in. There is a difference between hearing something and truly listening to it. You need to listen to what I'm saying."

"I do Tex, I promise. It's just harder to do, when you have no idea what the future will bring."

"That's why you need to follow your compass, kid. Trust it, and it will lead you in the right direction."

"I have since I met you. I just hope the magnet inside it works. But listen, to switch gears on you, I'm thinking of taking my girls to Cape Cod for Christmas weekend, I have them that week and I don't want to celebrate it here, no offense."

"None taken."
"Why don't you come with us? We'll get adjoining rooms, hang out by the indoor pool all day and find somewhere to have dinner. It will be fun."

"Thanks, but I can't. I have too much to do around here."
"What could you possible have to do around here on Christmas day? That's horse shit and you know it. You have a few days to decide, but I think it would be a lot of fun to get away."

"I'll think about it, how's that? But I usually spend Christmas helping out at the church and watching James Bond."

"Well, I think the Lord and 007 will understand if you skipped them this year. You're like family Tex and I don't want you to spend it alone. I'm booking a room for you."

"I don't know, maybe."
"I'm booking it."
The next week passed with the typical holiday cheer and music, along with spending money that you don't have, on gifts for people that don't need or deserve them. But because the retail stores perverted the meaning of Christmas, and came up with a great marketing campaign we all feel obligated to spend. I attended a few Christmas parties, enjoyed myself, and even somehow managed to be on the receiving end of oral sex performed by Jane. I gained the typical extra

weight from all the cookies, drinks and heavy pastas, and became annoyed every time I turned on the news, because there were always people arguing over political correctness, and the removal of a nativity scene somewhere. As if Jesus actually cares about an illumined plastic cut out of him on the lawn of a city hall, that gets stored in a basement, next to a furnace for the remaining ten months of the year.

"They are all fucking nuts," I repeated, "Both sides."

Christmas Eve morning had finally arrived, and I decided to place Santa's gifts for my children in the truck. As I was nearing completion, I heard the familiar sound of a rickety screen door shut and looked up. There Tex was, in all his glory, walking with his vintage army duffel bag towards my already running car. His bag was so old, it had actually come back into style. Tex carefully placed it in the trunk as to make sure he didn't damage the wrapped boxes.

"Thanks Hemingway, I needed this. I can't tell you the last time I enjoyed Christmas."

"I know pal, and thank you for coming. We'll have a blast."

We pulled up to my old house, beautifully decorated with all the figurines I had purchased over the years. I still remembered the day I had bought the sign that read " Reindeer Crossing" at the behest of my youngest, because she didn't want me to run over Rudolph. Of course my ex had to walk our very capable children to my car once again. As she reached my driver's side door, she tried to open it by pulling on the handle. I put down the window. "Can I help you?" I asked with a slight smirk. My ex decided to lecture me about several of the critical steps in child rearing, all of which were completely familiar and natural to me. After she rambled on like Charlie Brown's teacher for a few minutes, she said her good-byes to the girls.

"Bye mom, love you too."

The ride to the Cape took a little over an hour due to the snowfall. On the drive up, the girls got to know Tex. He told them several stories about his life growing up on a farm. They listened intently when he told a tale of how he helped dig Santa's sleigh out of the snow years before.

"Then we ate dinner together," he added.

"What did you have?" asked the older one.

"Pizza." Tex answered convincingly, as if he had actually eaten pizza with Santa that night.

Tex was always sharp tongued when it came to me, but he was a soft as a warm summer's breeze when he spoke to children. We soon arrived in Cape Cod and checked into our respective rooms. As I opened the door, both girls ran past me and began jumping on the beds, a ritual that I completely supported, and one that my ex strongly shunned. For that reason alone, I felt empowered watching my daughters enjoy their fleeting innocence.

"Lets go ladies, put your bathing suits on." It was Christmas Eve, and I wanted to go into town and attend the Christmas stroll that was taking place in a few hours along the harbor. The article in the paper said that the festival would be replete with more than fifty artists, stores open on Main Street, and that Christmas caroling would be performed by several local church groups. I asked my oldest to call Tex's room and let him know that we were heading to the pool. He abstained, but said he would be ready for the stroll. After about an hour of playing in the pool, we dried off and bundled up to face the snow that was still falling and accumulating with each passing minute.

When we arrived at the harbor, it was as if Norman Rockwell himself had painted the scenery. The snow covered lobster boats were tied up to the docks. A huge Christmas tree was decorated like Rockefeller Center, but unlike the farcical symbol in Times Square, this tree was still very much alive with it's roots planted firmly in the ground. This majestic Spruce isn't destined to end up rotting in a landfill the week after Christmas. No, someone with common sense had planted a sapling years ago in the middle of the crescent shaped common alongside the ocean. In the field, there were many different artists selling all types of goods in three sided gazebos. In the rear, a parked vintage VW bus was selling coffee and hot chocolate. That caught the attention of Tex and the girls while the carolers were singing "Deck the Halls" for all to hear. After a quick walk and giving in to the elements, we decided on the warmth of hot cocoa and coffee. As we stood in front of the cow painted van, I ordered and paid for two coffees and two hot chocolates. We grasped the hot cups with both hands and began to walk around the Norman Rockwell landscape. We wandered into a few of the local artists' cabins and looked at the pieces for sale. They were the typical fare one finds in a seaside town. Paintings and pictures of lighthouses and empty beach chairs, funny quotes about being a beach bum, and sea glass with driftwood sculptures. After about half an hour, Tex and I gave in to the girls' persistence and crossed Main Street to enter a toy store. It was an independent store that competed with the big box warehouses that lacked soul, and sold everything from toilet paper to guns. As soon as we opened the old wooden door of the quaint store, the smell of popcorn permeated the air. I knew I was a defeated man as we traversed the aisles filled with bright toys and stuffed animals. Tex walked over to the machine and filled a bag with free popcorn. Both girls quickly selected a toy and made their way to the register. Just as I was reaching into my pocket to pay the gentleman behind the counter, Tex came over and handed him his credit card.

"On me kid"
"No, please, I got it."
Tex just looked at me with his blue eyes surrounded by crows' feet not saying a word, but saying everything. His silence was deafening. I quickly realized that I wasn't about to win this argument. "Girls, say thank you to Tex," I said as I stepped back.

They both said thank you and followed it up with a double hug that Tex happily accepted.

"Thanks Tex," I said, with a humbled inflection in my voice.

As we walked out of the store, both girls played with their new toys while Tex continued to eat his popcorn. We waited on the snow covered sidewalk for the jolly policeman wearing a Santa hat to safely cross us back to the common. Once there, we wandered into a few more artist gazebos. As I passed one, I stopped dead in my snow covered tracks. I couldn't believe what I was seeing. Telling the others to hold up, I walked inside, where I noticed a woman sitting behind a small desk with a space heater next to her quilt covered legs, reading a book.

"Excuse me ma'am?"
"Yes?" She lifted her head exposing a genuine smile along with eyes that housed love for the universe.

"I was curious about that picture you have hanging up outside."
"Which one?"
"The one with the lone tree on the beach, with the ocean in the background."

"I named it Solitude and Strength. What questions do you have about it?"
"Where was it taken?"
"I captured that on the beach last summer in Wellfleet."
"That's incredible. I took an almost identical picture years ago in Mexico. I'm stunned to see one just like it." Always the self-defeatist, I added that her picture was much nicer.

"Really?" answered Mary.

"Yes, I can't believe it. What are the odds? . . . Hi, my name is Hemingway, James, Hemingway, no relation to the author."

"I'm Mary, no relation to the savior."

"Ha! Good one. You look much too young anyways," I said. Tex being the former snake eater that he was, picked up on the immediate attraction and quickly introduced himself. After a short conversation, he bribed the kids with a ride on the carrousel located in front of the Christmas tree.

"Are those your children?" asked Mary.

"Yes they are. I'm sorry I didn't make an introduction, but they wanted to ride the horses."

"No need for an explanation, James." I noticed right away that she called me by my first name, a gesture I was not accustomed to. We continued our conversation about the picture without an audience.

"Your girls are adorable, James. You're a lucky man."

"It's funny you say that Mary because it wasn't until recently, that I realized just how truly lucky I am."

"Why do you say that James?"

Since we didn't have all night to converse and wanting the dialogue to remain light, I provided a watered down, Cliff note version of events that had lead me to this place.

"Do you think all those twists and turns were supposed to happen to help guide you on a specific path?"

"I never used to, but now I do."
"We have all had our fair share of hardships James, but it's how you survive them that makes your story unique." Mary led him outside to look at the picture in question. "You said you took the same picture?"

"Yes, well, not quite, but it's uncanny how similar the two pictures are. I am by no means an artist, but that tree spoke to me that day years ago. Oddly enough, besides a picture of my kids, it's one of the few things I took with me when I moved out. I have no clue why, but it's always been present in my life, like I have some sort of odd connection with it. And here I am looking at the exact same picture."

"Why do you think that is, James?"
"Honestly, up until a few months ago I would have chalked it up to nothing more than a random occurrence in an even more random world, but now I'm starting to feel like the universe talks to us, and it's our responsibility to listen."

"What's it saying to you?"
"I don't want to creep you out but maybe I was supposed to meet you. Maybe that picture I took was the lighthouse guiding me though the storms of my life. Maybe that picture led me to right here, right now."

"I don't believe in coincidences either James," Mary said with a grin on her beautifully natural face.

"Why did you name it Strength and Solitude?"
"One needs to be strong to stand alone, to weather the storms that come and go throughout life. Sometimes you don't see what's right in front of you James."

"Were you that tree, Mary?"
"I was for far too long James, and I, like that tree, withstood the storms alone, and the strength I speak of isn't just physical James; it's also mental."

"I'm that tree now." I responded quietly. By this time, an older couple had walked in, and begun to admire a few pieces of art located on the shelf behind the counter. Mary excused herself with the grace of a European queen from a time since past and offered her assistance. The older woman asked about a specific bowl made from pottery that was on display behind where Mary was originally sitting.

"I've never seen anything like that before; it's beautiful. Is that real gold?"
"I wish it was, but no, gold is much too expensive now. That one is copper, but this small one here is made from gold," Mary said, as she handed the woman a small clay bowl about the size of a teacup. Mary went on to explain that the form of pottery was called Kintsukuroi. "You take a beautiful object

and then you break it. Just when you think it's worthless and needs to be discarded, you solder all the pieces back to the original form using gold. The cracks then transform into the most attractive part of the bowl; the scars are the reason why the bowl becomes so beautiful."

The woman's husband then summarized, "So, the bowl becomes more beautiful after it has been broken and then mended . . . interesting."

"That bowl was once ordinary and plain, but now it has become distinguished and one of a kind as well. There will never be another bowl like that one; each one breaks differently." Mary added.

"The gentleman commented, "I guess you could apply that same logic to a person that has been broken."

"I guess you could," Mary replied, subtly winking at me, letting me know that that was exactly the meaning behind the bowls. Mary, being the honest person that she was, explained to the couple that she had been the one broken, feeling nearly useless, but she had repaired the cracks in her life, and that's what had made her stronger and unique.

"Good for you." the woman said with assertive compassion. The small sticker on the bowl listed the price at six hundred dollars. The gentleman in the Burberry scarf wearing a paperboy hat offered her five hundred, cash. She gladly accepted his offer with a handshake, wrapped the bowl in last week's newspaper and placed it in a small paper bag with twine handles. As Mary thanked them for her only sale that evening the man replied, "Nonsense, we thank you. You gave us a life lesson, and that's no small feat coming from someone my age. This bowl is for my daughter, who is going through a difficult time right now. This is exactly what I need to show her, that even though she has scars, that's what gives her strength and makes her beautiful. "So for that, I thank you Mary," he said as he tipped his hat good bye.

The woman, feeling a bond with Mary, gave her a hug. As she was walking out with bag in hand, she stopped and turned towards me, having no idea I had just met Mary twenty minutes prior, and said, "You have a very special woman right there, don't be a fool."

"I promise, I won't," I said. Then, looking at Mary, I commented, "Quite a double entendre you have there."

"I've repaired myself like I did those bowls James. Now I think it's your turn, but don't forget, it's the cracks that make us special, so we stand out in a crowd. Life is like pottery James, the bigger the break, the more beautiful it can become once repaired."

I just stared at Mary with a look of vulnerability on my face, exposing my fragmented heart. Excusing myself to check on Tex and my daughters, I noticed him standing between the two girls who were sitting on painted horses circling the carousel. Tex noticed that I was looking in his direction and gave me the thumbs up, only to disappear with the rotation of the ride.

It was quarter 'til seven and the Christmas stroll concluded in fifteen minutes. Mary asked me what my plans were for the rest of Christmas Eve.

"Not too much," I replied. We'll probably just go try to find a place to eat, head back to the hotel and call it a night. I'm sure the girls will get me up at the crack of dawn."

"That's precious James; you're a good man. There isn't much open tonight. I was just going to order some take out and head home myself. There's an electric blanket and a glass of cabernet waiting for me."

"I hope I'm not being too forward, but why don't you come eat with us?
"Thanks, but you should spend the time with your girls, James. There is always the future."

"Come on, it will be fun. Tex and the girls won't care. It's Christmas, and you're not spending it alone."

The cold weather and Tex's susceptibility to motion sickness won out over the girls' enthusiasm. After the third ride, all three made their way back to Mary's gazebo. When I informed my girls that Mary was going to join us for dinner, they both instantaneously argued over who was going to get to sit next to her. "I guess that settles it then, Mary."

"Can you tell us the story of the mermaid that lives out there?" the little one asked as she pointed to the water. Tex winked at Mary while standing behind the girls.

"Of course I can. I've seen her several times," Mary said while looking at Tex. I'll tell you the story at dinner."

"Yay!"
"The only place that I can think of, that would be open is the Chinese buffet at the end of Main St.
"Perfect, we'll meet you there in an hour."

"Sounds great, I just have to lock up, I don't think anyone else is coming in tonight."

As I walked away, I heard Mary call out my name. Turning around, I saw her jogging over to me holding an object in her hand. "Here, I want you to have this," she said, handing me Strength and Solitude. I didn't refuse and thanked her with a "very much," accompanied by a much needed, warm embrace.

Even though we had agreed to meet in an hour, we both arrived twenty minutes early. The hostess sat us at the table closest to the buffet, just as Tex had requested. "Why on

Gods green Earth would anyone want to sit away from the food? makes no sense." Tex said to the amusement of the Oriental hostess. While walking to the table I assured the girls that they each could sit next to Mary. The food was surprisingly good, other than the fact that the pizza tasted exactly like a pizza should taste at a Chinese buffet. Mary told the girls fantastical tales of mermaids and pirates living in the waters off Cape Cod. After dinner she brought the girls up to the self serve ice cream machine. Both came back with sundaes that resembled the leaning tower of Pisa with jimmies. Mary brought a much smaller one back to the table and placed it in front of the adults for all to share. "I picked swirl because I didn't know what flavors you gentleman liked," she explained.

"That's perfect "I told her.
"Ugh, no thanks," Tex said as he rubbed his over gorged stomach. "I shouldn't have had that last serving, I'm gonna burst."

"Yeah, I thought the sixth plate would have been enough for you," I chided.

I reached in first with my stainless steel spoon and scooped equal parts vanilla and chocolate. Mary teasingly removed the contents from my spoon as I lifted it from the bowl. She then picked up the fallen ice cream with her spoon and ate it, causing smiles all around. The check came and Tex grabbed it at the displeasure of both Mary and I.

"Put your money away. It's my Christmas present."

"Thanks grandpa" I replied.

Mary rose from her chair and walked over to Tex, "Thank you," she said, as she hugged the side of his neck while he remained sitting.

"Yeah, yeah, yeah."

Though I dreaded it, the dinner had to come to an end. I still had to get back to the room to make sure Santa brought the toys for the girls. Mary carried the little one to the car and buckled her in, then turned around and hugged the oldest. "You take care of your daddy, ok?"

"Ok, I promise."

"Thanks Mary, I said sincerely."

"For what?"

"For being so nice to my kids. I always get nervous telling people that I have two children because I never know how they will take it."

"James, if someone doesn't want you for your children, then they don't deserve one minute of your time. Kids add value, not subtract it."

"I know, but it still was so nice to see you treat them the way you did."

"It was my pleasure James. I hope I get to see them again."

"Really? I would love that Mary."

"Do you think it was just a coincidence that we met tonight?"
"What do you think James?"
"I truly feel that the universe brought us together. Some type of energy attracted us like magnets. Does that sound insane to you?"

"Magnets aren't always metal, James"
"I'm starting to believe that Mary."
Tex rolled down the window. "Are you two love birds ready?"
"Sorry Tex," I said. Good night Mary. It was truly a pleasure meeting you."
"Yes it was James," Mary replied as she gave me her hand-made business card. "Make sure you call."

"I promise I will," I said over the roof of my car. "Good night"
    Back at the hotel the girls readied for bed, putting their pajamas on and brushing their teeth. Outside, Tex was unloading the toys from the trunk while bitching about his back.

"Are you sure Santa will find us daddy?"
"Of course honey. Remember when we went to the mall and you told him that we were staying here. What did he say to you?"

"He said that he wouldn't forget because we were really goods girls this year."

"Exactly honey, I promise he will come."

The mall Santa was a professional, immediately picking up on what the little girl was saying, and assured her that he would be there.

As soon as the girls fell asleep, I called Tex's adjoining room and let him know that the coast was clear. Although there was no Christmas tree, I was sure that the excitement of unwrapping the gifts would supersede the realization that the gifts were on a small round table and not under a plastic, flame retardant tree.

A few hours later the girls awoke with the usual reckless abandon that accompanies Christmas morning as they found the gifts.

"He didn't forget daddy!"
"I told you, kiddo."

Tex was already on his third cup of coffee when the girls awoke. I called his room and Tex walked though the adjoining door with cup in hand, his eyes lit up with magic, just like the girls who were already opening their presents.

"Come look what Santa brought," the youngest one yelled to Tex.
"Coming honey"
"This is what it's all about kid, remember that." Tex said to me.
"You're right."
"Don't ever forget how you feel right now." Tex said, as he walked over to the girls and sat on the chair next to the table.

After the girls played with their new toys and took a quick dip in the indoor pool, we packed up and headed back home. On the way, I called Mary and thanked her for a lovely evening, wished her a very merry Christmas, and told her that I hoped Santa had been good to her.

"Say hello to Mary, girls." I held the phone up and pointed it in the direction of the back seat.

"Hi Mary! Merry Christmas!" they yelled, out of sync."

I dropped the girls off along with all of Santa's gifts, knowing full well that I would never see them again. But I also knew that the girls had a playroom at their mom's house and I wouldn't have been able to fit all the toys in the cabin. As soon as the front door closed and the girls were safely inside, I began to speak of Mary.
"I can't believe that picture Tex. Mine was taken in Mexico ten years ago, and hers on the Cape last summer. What are the odds?"

"Slim, to none, and Slim just left town on his horse. So don't screw it up. That's the universe talking to you, you're finally listening."

Tex then told me the story of the man in the flood.
"A massive flood rushes a small town one day, and as the waters began to rise, a man in a house managed to climb on his roof to escape the elevating waters. As the water became

more violent, his neighbor placed a ladder up against his house, and yelled for him climb down so they could escape. The man replied, "No, I prayed to God for protection, and my God will save me from the rising waters." The man then removed his ladder and moved on to save his neighbors. A few minutes later, the water level had risen further and a man pulled up in a boat. "Jump" he said, and I'll save you. Again, the man replied, "No, The lord, my Savior will protect me from the flood." So the man left to rescue other people that were trapped. About an hour later the waters had neared the roof of the dwelling and continued to rise. Finally a helicopter flew overhead and dropped a basket. The man sitting in the open door yelled to him over the roar of the blades, "Climb in or you'll be swept away." Again, the man replied, "No, my God will protect me, go save someone else." The rapid waters continued to rise and swept the man away. Soon after his demise, he was greeted by St. Peter, who welcomed him with open arms into Heaven. Very disappointed, the man approached God and asked, "Why did you forsake me? I prayed everyday of my life; my faith in you was never compromised. I lived my life as a good man. Why didn't you didn't save me?"

God replied, "My foolish son, I sent you a neighbor with a ladder, a man in a boat and a helicopter with a basket. What more did you want me to do?"
"The point being, Hemingway, God sends people to save us. Make sure you don't push them away like the knucklehead on the roof."

"I get it now Tex, and I won't this time."

As soon as Tex was finished telling me about the universe and how it will conspire to guide us in life, the phone rang. I looked at the caller ID, hoping it was Mary and not a bill collector. "Hello Mary" I said. We spoke briefly and Mary thanked me again for a wonderful dinner and asked about the girls' morning. We made tentative plans to see each other soon.

"Good bye Mary."
"Good bye James."

As soon as I walked in the door, I removed Strength and Solitude out of a white disposable bag along with some fudge from the candy store. I placed it next to my picture to compare the two. Even though there were minor discrepancies, the pictures were virtually the same.

I had never been a big drinker and couldn't recall the last time I'd enjoyed one by myself, but for some reason I felt that this moment called for such an event. I poured myself two fingers worth of a surprisingly good local whiskey, walked out onto the porch and sat down on the cold wooden chair. Before long, the whiskey warmed my soul, and my body temperature warmed the chair. As I looked up into the heavens, I noticed that there wasn't a cloud in the sky and was easily able to locate my favorite constellation with ease. That loyal cluster of stars had been witness to every important event in my life, never wavering in its unbiased presence. I found great comfort in knowing that those stars would be there, shining brightly from light years away, until I no longer existed, and joined them. I was completely submerged in my thoughts, no longer aware of my surroundings, but having an internal dialogue with whomever was listening. Myself? God? Perhaps the universe . . . or no one at all. I thought of my life, the triumphs and pitfalls, the birth of my children and the unknown future that lies ahead. Was it truly a higher power's hand that had led me to the cabins? The desire to take another sip of my whiskey snapped me out of the trance. I refocused my eyes and noticed that it had begun to snow. I compared not knowing my future, to the stars above. Both provided an infinite number of possibilities. I didn't need to see an outline of Jesus on a burnt piece of toast to confirm my faith. I was sure that a higher power was out there somewhere. I stood up, took in the last mouthful of whiskey and walked inside. There, I readied myself and laid down to bed. I thought of everything someone *shouldn't* think about when trying to sleep, but I couldn't help it. I was depressed. Nonetheless I was confident that the stars above would watch over me tonight like vigilant soldiers, and knowing this brought me the much needed protection in realizing that everything would be all right.

CHAPTER 11

---◆---

Hope Dies Last

OVER THE NEXT few weeks, Mary and I communicated regularly, always phone calls, never text messages. Mary despised that form of unattached communication and deferred to handwritten letters even more. She would say that penning a letter exposed the author's soul, sometimes even revealing the location of fallen teardrops on the paper. That weekend I brought my children to the stationary store where I purchased high quality paper so as to begin using that form of communication, along with butterfly and heart shaped stamps for the girls. In the first sentence of the first letter that I penned, I apologized for my sloppy penmanship and terrible spelling, also for scribbling the letter with a free pen from the bank, instead of a fountain pen like the one she uses to scribe.

Mary invited me to the Cape the following weekend. I immediately made reservations online and arrived at my hotel lobby around eight pm on Friday night. Mary was already there waiting on the navy blue couch, reading a flyer about an historic train ride along the coast. She stood up and embraced me. "Have you ever done one of these?"
"Once in New Hampshire with the kids, but no, not here."

"Ok, let's do this sometime."

"Sounds great, I'd love to." I was more excited about the fact that Mary was planning future dates, than I was about the impending motion sickness I would surely acquire during the ride. We walked up to the woman at the counter and I checked in. I refused Mary's offer to pay and handed the woman my credit card. The universe had brought us together and I wasn't about to let a minimum payment on an already maxed out credit card stop me.

It was early February and the weather on the New England coast brought with it the wet snow and gray skies that I despised. Mary held onto my left arm as we navigated the slippery streets to the restaurant where she had made reservations. The hostess brought us to a table that overlooked the cold dark ocean. Mary told me that she always seized the opportunity to look out at the ocean no matter what the season. I agreed, telling her about my belief in the medicinal power out there. "Not sure what it is, but it makes me feel better too," I commented.

"Your body is more than half water James; there's something to that."

Just then the waiter walked over and brought a wine menu. I looked briefly and on the waiter's recommendation, ordered an expensive bottle of red from the Californian coast.

"I hope you like what I picked."

"I'm sure I will James, I just like your assertiveness."

The waiter returned moments later with the bottle and poured a small amount in one glass for me to taste, but I instructed the waiter to hand the glass to Mary. "Would you like to smell the cork?" the waiter asked me.

"Uh, no thanks, that won't be necessary. Mary, would you like to smell the cork?" I inquired with a smile.

"No thank you, I smelt one earlier and I'm all corked out," she quipped.
All three of us laughed at the pompous request. Then the waiter said, "I have to ask or I'll get in trouble."

"No, I know, we were just joking," I assured him.
"It's refreshing to wait on people like you. Enjoy your wine, and I'll be back shortly to take your order."

He filled both our glasses and walked away from the table. Mary then informed me that the ocean was one of the reasons why she moved to the Cape.

"What is the other one Mary?"
"My life" Mary said shortly, as she gingerly swirled her wine.
"Do you want to share it with me?"
"Sure. Enough time has passed where it is just a distant memory, but I didn't have a good one."

"What? A life?" I asked.

"Yes, a life." Mary explained that her grandfather was a sea captain here on the Cape many moons ago. "My mother married my father who was stationed in upstate New York. That's where I was raised but I always had a calling to the sea. Maybe it's in my blood."

"You told me it was, Mary."
"I think you're right, James."
"I married right out of college to a boy from a prominent family out there. At first it was fun and I was enamored by the galas and bright lights, but that spoiled as fast as an opened bottle of champagne. I knew I was living a lie. I was surrounded by people who cared only about Ivy League schools and money. I always felt that those people looked down on me. They looked though me, not at me."

"Would your ex have smelled that cork?" I asked jokingly.
"Ugh, totally" she answered laughingly.
I would go to the opera but all I wanted was to be at a reggae concert. I would be forced to attend five thousand dollar a plate dinners just so he could pose for pictures next to some politician, but all I wanted was some Mexican food. He was a good man, my husband, but he was handicapped, not physically, but mentally. He lived a spoiled life of nannies and country clubs, and lacked the ability to handle life's stressors because his parents always fixed everything with money. It's very important to teach your children the value of money and set boundaries, two aspects of his childhood that were lacking. His mother was an alcoholic and his

father was never around, so he replaced love with inanimate objects. I was one of those objects to him, nothing more than a toy truck or a ball. I was a silenced woman who had the appearance of a great life, but it was all lies. Things came to a head when we found out that I couldn't have children. Instead of being supportive of my inability to conceive, he became enraged like I had something to do with it. My body said no to him, and it triggered something primal from his childhood, a childhood where "no" was never an option. That next morning I packed a bag with a handful of my belongings, hopped a cab to the train station, and made my way to the sea. He tracked me down in attempts to repair the relationship but I knew he didn't have the tools. His parents made sure there was a prenup so I received nothing, but honestly James, I wanted nothing from them. I just wanted to leave."

"Wow Mary, it takes a very strong woman to do that. You should be proud of yourself."

"Thank you James."
"Well, we won't need a prenup because between us we have about a hundred dollars," I said to lighten the mood.

"I wouldn't want it any other way James, truly perfect."
Mary continued, "When I arrived I had a bag of clothes and a pocket full of dreams. I pawned my wedding ring for less than half of its value and found a cute little cottage within walking distance of the beach, so here I am James."

"I'm glad you're here, Mary."

"I am too, but you know what's funny James? The fact that I'm more happy now - only owning the essentials and driving my nineteen eighty three VW rabbit - than I was when I lived in a castle, driving a car with a heated steering wheel."

"Wow, they make heated steering wheels?" I asked, honestly never having heard that such an option was available on certain types of cars.

"James, you are too funny."

"I'm actually being serious, I had no idea that even existed. I guess Toyota didn't feel like putting it in my car in two thousand and six."

"I still remember sitting in my VW for the first time. Those uncomfortable seats felt so right, the two FM radio stations sounded perfect, and every time I touch that freezing cold, plastic steering wheel, it reminds me of what I left behind, and some how that coldness makes me proud. It sounds dumb I know."

"No it doesn't Mary. Trust me, I get it," I said, raising my glass to make a toast. "To cold steering wheels."

"To cold steering wheels." Mary repeated.

I then told her my story, realizing that she was the first woman I had met with whom I felt safe sharing the details. I felt no reason to white wash or omit the embarrassing aspects of my past, though I didn't find it necessary to inform her about the Russian that had used me a few months prior, so I left that part out. I proudly told her about the cabin and all its "character" as she so delicately put it. "That's one way to look at it, I said." I spoke of Tex in great length and how he had saved my life more than once.

"You're lucky to have found him, James."

I let her know about the omens that had created the path for me lately and how I now believed that the universe conspires to navigate us though the rough waters of life.

"It's difficult to tell you, but I remember my ex always making fun of me when I wanted to sit outside and look at the stars, kind of like your cold steering wheel. Now when I look up and dream, I'm defying her; I'm taking my power back."

"Yes you are James, yes you are." Mary said as she raised her glass now, and made a toast.

"To cold steering wheels and gazing at the stars."
"I just smiled and replied "Amen to that."
The rest of the weekend went as well as the dinner that had started it. Both mornings Mary met me in the lobby. From there, we walked to the coffee shop around the corner. As luck or fate would have it, both mornings we were able to sit at the table directly in front of the fireplace with actual wood burning, instead of the ones that required a light switch

on the wall. Mary ordered green tea while I kept with my tradition of asking for the darkest roast available. We walked arm in arm on the frozen sand of the beach when I noticed a beautiful seashell. I picked it up and handed the shell to Mary. We continued down the beach, coming across another shell even more beautiful than the last. I picked this one up and placed it in Mary's hand with the previous one. This happened several times during the stroll.

"They are just like life James."
Not understanding what she meant by her comment, I asked, "What's like life?"

"The shells in my hand that you just handed me James. When you first started to walk on the beach, you quickly came upon the most beautiful shell. You walked another twenty feet and found another, better than the first. Look at all the shells you handed me. They created a path that lead you to this one right here." She showed me, holding up the last one, in between her thumb and forefinger. There will always be a perfect shell for you James. You just have to look for it. The path of the shells you chose, have brought you to this shell because it was meant for you. Someone else would have chosen a different one for different reasons. Maybe it's the different shapes, or different colors - just like life James. Those seashells are like a boulevard of life that led you here."

"Sea shells and magnets - the keys to life. Who would have thought?" I commented.

Each night ended in the same fashion. I would walk Mary to her front door, receive a hug and kiss on the cheek in return. It was clear that we both wanted more, but for the sake of a healthy respect for one another, we showed restraint.

I returned to Rhode Island to an inquisitive Tex who showed up at my cabin moments after my car appeared in the driveway. Even though it was Sunday night, Tex still wanted to drink his caffeinated coffee while he listened to stories from the weekend. I put on decaf without informing him because Tex thought as much of decaf as he did of non-alcoholic beer.

"What's the point?" he would ask.

I knew better, so I kept the Santa lie to myself and as soon as the decaf coffee was done brewing, poured two cups and walked outside to an old man sitting on a cold wooden chair.

"So how did it go this weekend? Any different than your other first dates?"
"The weekend was perfect, Tex. I mean I couldn't have asked for anything better. She's not only the nicest person I've ever met, but she has a story too."

"We all do, kid, don't ever forget that."
"I'm staring to figure that out. It was just so refreshing to go on a date with a woman who didn't post a picture of her

drink on social media or text her friends all night long. We didn't even kiss all weekend and to be honest, Tex, I'm glad we didn't."

"You didn't kiss her?"
"Nope, didn't even try to, not that she would have accepted, but it just felt right not to rush things."

"That makes sense, I guess."
"I was starting to lose faith in women, Tex. I mean some girls will give you a blowjob but won't have sex with you. Others will have sex with you, but won't give a blowjob. What kind of perverse moral codes do these people live by?"

"We're all screwed up kid, even you and I, but don't even try to figure that shit out."

"I know we are Tex, but it's just refreshing to meet someone less screwed up then we are."

"Good point" Tex said. "As long as she isn't as crazy as a buzzard on the back of a shit wagon, you should be fine."

"I don't think she is."
"But don't forget the only reason why the grass is always greener on the other side of the fence."

"What reason's that?"

"Because there's more horse shit on the other side. If you find the right girl, don't look over that fence, because once you get that horse shit on the bottom of your shoe, you're screwed kid."

"Very true," I said, amazed at the simplistic analogies Tex used to explain so many of life's important lessons and pitfalls.

"Anyways, she's divorced and can't have kids. Her ex is some spoiled brat from upstate New York and, get this, she also believes in omens and that the universe has a soul - all of that path of life stuff that you taught me."

"That's great, she seemed like a great girl."
"She is, but I'm just scared Tex. I mean, I think I already like this woman and my heart can't take another crack. I was actually giving up hope that I would ever find the right one."

"Hope dies last."
"What?"
Tex repeated himself, but this time slower, while he placed an emphasis on the end of each word. "Hope, dies, last. Do you think all of us in those God forsaken foxholes ever gave up hope? Even when we were out gunned and out flanked, we never gave up hope, because once that thought creeps into your head, it's over. You can't get it out, trust me kid."

"I do Tex, I trust what you say whole heartedly. You've helped me though so much with your advice and words of wisdom. You're the only one I can talk to."

"Alright, alright, don't get all sentimental on me now, you pussy."

I responded, "Don't get me wrong, you're still a miserable son of a bitch, but you're a helpful one."

"Better" Tex replied, appreciating the joke directed at him.

"I know it sounds corny, but years ago I would see the slush on the ground as nothing more than a nuisance, just one of the many pitfalls of the winter season, but now because of that same sludge from the colon of Mr. Winter himself, I was able to hold Mary's arm the whole time we walked around. I guess I'm just starting to look at things a bit differently now."

"What's your favorite food?" asked Tex.

"Uh, I guess pizza or maybe a cheeseburger," I said with a confused look on my face.

"Ok, have you ever had a shitty burger before?" inquired Tex.

"Yeah, I guess so."

"Did it stop you from ordering a burger again?"

"No"

"Exactly. Just because you ate a terrible burger on a few occasions throughout the course of your life, doesn't mean that all burgers at all restaurants suck. Even the same restaurant you ate the shitty burger at, most likely serves great burgers, but the cook screwed up. That doesn't make him a bad cook; he just messed up your order once. You can't give up on all burgers, because one sucked. Don't be afraid to order that burger again, kid. Remember, the best chef in the world will burn a piece of chicken once in a while."

I once again knew exactly what Tex was preaching, and appreciated the simplicity with which he presented it.

"So how did you guys leave it off?"
"Hopefully she comes down, but I gave her the option. It's up to her."
"That's great. Just don't fuck it up Hemingway. She might be the best burger you'll ever have. Alright kid, I'm getting tired, good night."

As Tex walked away, he turned back towards me as I was picking up the cups and said, "The world doesn't come to you, Hemingway; you need to go after it."

I put the mugs back down on the red cooler, and sat by myself in the comfortable winter air and looked at the stars above. I inhaled and held my breath until my body informed me that enough time had passed. I exhaled and laughed out loud to no one. He's right again I thought to myself. How could he equate the most difficult and emotional aspect of my life to a fucking cheeseburger and make complete sense?

I couldn't recall many memories of my late grandmother, but the one I could always conjure up when I cast my memory back, was of the time she told me that the stars were holes in heaven's floor. It dawned on me that perhaps that was the place from which my fondness for the universe and the great unknown had developed. How I wished that my grandmother's interpretation was the truth. If stars really were the holes from which heaven's light shined through, then I wouldn't have to worry about the course of my life here on earth. Things would be so much easier knowing that the guiding lights would keep me on the right path and wait for my eternal embrace. But unlike a college freshman returning home after his first semester, eating a home cooked meal and getting his laundry done by his mother, heaven wasn't awaiting. Faith, and faith alone guarantees a heaven. My faith was not absolute. I wished it was, but it wasn't. It had ebbed and flowed throughout my life. I also knew, however, that my God was all loving and would allow for my doubting too.

The days and weeks that followed were largely as mundane as the ones prior. Each morning the alarm went off at exactly 6:02am, and yes, I would tell people who asked, "Those two minutes do make a difference." Go to the gym, head to work, stop at the same coffee shop, see the same people there, work for about nine hours while only getting paid for eight, fill the void of the night with a book - or some brain rotting program on the television, and repeat. Now, however, my days were punctuated with much anticipated conversations with Mary. The monotony of the assembly line day no longer ruled, I now had a reason to better myself, and that reason was Mary.

When Mary indicated that she could come to Rhode Island the following weekend, I gladly encouraged her to do so. For better or worse, she was going to see where I lived, but one good thing about living in a cabin the size of a dorm room was the fact that it was very easy to clean. This place was so small that I could practically turn off the bathroom light from my bed. I cleaned the countertops and Chico's table, scrubbed the bathroom and waxed the hardwood floors. I even swept the miniature golf carpet on the front porch. As Tex would say to me more than once when I would complain about the cabin's water pressure, "You can't make chicken soup, out of chicken shit, kid." I did, however, go out and purchase seven hundred thread count sheets for the bed, a significant improvement from the bed in a bag I'd originally bought for twenty dollars.

CHAPTER 12

------------ ⚜ ------------

Save Tex from the Tax Man

ON THE MORNING of Mary's arrival, the cabin was spotless, lopsided and dated, but spotless. I lit the organic candle I had purchased with the sheets. Since I couldn't find recently divorced scent, I'd settled on fresh cotton. Just as I was feeling that sense of accomplishment over a clean house, I heard a knock on the door. Mary wasn't supposed to arrive for another two hours, I figured it must be Tex. I opened the door and sure enough, in walked Tex.

"Smells like a laundromat in here."
"Looks good, doesn't it?" I asked with pride. "Want some coffee?"
"Well, I'm not here to claim a winning lottery ticket. Do you have anymore of those Stella Doro cookie things left?"

"Let me check, have a seat." I sensed that Tex was more ornery than usual.
"What's wrong pal? You don't seem yourself today."
"Ahh, nothing, just the usual horse shit from the government."

"Talk to me goose, I'm here." I said, referencing the movie Top Gun as every man in his early forties does a few times a year.

"I just got my tax bill and they're going up again. I can't believe it! What do they do with all this money?"

Tex backed up his irate tone with knowing the State's budget and comparing it to twenty years ago.
"It's gone up a thousand percent! My property hasn't grown, let alone increased in value. My trash doesn't get picked up more often, the cops and firemen haven't been here in years, not since that standoff more than a decade ago."

"What standoff?
"I don't know, some guy from Abilene. The point is that I can't afford this place anymore; I'm going to lose it soon."

"Well, we'll figure something out Tex. How can I help?"
"You can't kid. I just don't know what I'm going to do, that's all. But enough of this bullshit though - let's change the subject,"
Tex said, he always disliked dwelling on negative inevitabilities.

"Can you tell me about the standoff then?"
"I don't know. He escaped from prison and was on the run. He was a nice enough guy. We had a handful of beers together and talked about the war, he was infantry. He did

something stupid years ago when he was a kid. He thought twenty-two years was long enough to spend in prison so he decided to leave, but the warden and the State had a difference of opinion. I didn't know him as a kid, but the man that I met shouldn't have been incarcerated. Too bad the government didn't think so. So many tax dollars are wasted on paying for rehabilitated people to rot in prison cells."

I brought the coffee and plastic package of cookies over to Chico's table.
"I can't do this anymore James."
I immediately picked up on the fact that Tex used my first name. He had always referred to me as kid or Hemingway, but never James. I was actually surprised that Tex even remembered what my first name was.

"What can't you do?"
"This, this place. I can't do it anymore. I have enough money for the next quarter's taxes but after that, I have no clue what I'm going to do."

"We'll figure something out, Tex. You've always been there for me, and I'm here for you."

"Thanks Hemingway." Back to the last name; Tex must be feeling better I mused.

"Why are the taxes so high here? Does the tax man see something that I don't see?"

"I think they are trying to force me to sell out to one of those developers. Plus, I just heard the other night from Misty that some big developer with his own television show from New York just bought up all the farmland across the street and is starting to build a hotel, condo thing. Something like two hundred units with a couple of fancy restaurants, and get this, a friggin' pool on the roof. That bastard will get a tax credit but I can't. I wonder what war he fought in. Ha!" Tex huffed, as he scoffed at the irony.

"Tex, if there's one thing I know for certain about you, it's that you're a survivor. Look at what the universe has thrown at you, and you've survived. It will conspire to help you, I just know it will."

"The universe better start conspiring soon because the clock is ticking kid," Tex responded.

"Remember the quote from Churchill you told me a while back?"
"Which one?"
"If you're going through hell, keep going." You told me that Tex. Now it's your turn to listen to every ounce of the great advice you have given me over the past few months."

Tex had enough melancholic talk for the day. "So why does this place smell like a laundry mat anyway?"

"Mary is coming down for a few days and I didn't want to wait for housekeeping."

"Oh, that's right, they've been on vacation for a while."
"Make sure I get to say hello to her, and make sure you take her somewhere nice tonight. Any girl willing to stay here deserves a decent meal."

"Already made reservations at The Wharf tonight, pal."
"Whoa, excuse me, I didn't know you robbed a bank," Tex replied, knowing that it was the nicest place in town. I still remember the time I took my Anne there. I can still see the look on her face and taste the wine from that night, and it's been twenty years. Try to get the table in front of the fireplace."

"Already did."
"How the hell did you pull that off? That table is usually reserved for Senators and blue bloods."

"I went in and spoke to the host yesterday. I told him it was our anniversary, that, and I slipped him sixty bucks during the handshake."

"Money makes the world go 'round, good for you kid."
As late afternoon approached, I was clean-shaven and prepared. I debated whether to leave my five o'clock shadow or shave it, but after hearing from my oldest over the phone that

I was more handsome without it, I shaved. After Tex left for the V.F.W., I went to the local florist and bought a bouquet of my favorite flowers in hopes that Mary had similar tastes. Sunflowers, always sunflowers. I wasn't aware of one room that couldn't be brightened by their presence, plus they were a safe bet, without any color codes for love or friendship, just beautiful flowers to make a beautiful girl smile. Next to the flower shop, was a boutique wine store where I bought a bottle each of red and white at the suggestion of the attractive, recently divorced woman behind the counter.

"Better off being on the safe side," she said, while letting me know how lucky that woman must be, having such a handsome man buying her flowers and wine. "I'm the lucky one," I corrected. She baited the hook, but I didn't bite. I'd bitten that hook one too many times and learned my lesson. I thanked her for the advice on the selection and walked out.

I was sitting at Chico's table reading a book on the fall of the Roman Empire, starting to notice that today's government was becoming yesterday's Rome, when I heard the distinct sound of sporadic stones shifting underneath the weight of a car slowly approaching my cabin. I walked to the door, wiped my palms on my jeans a couple of times to remove any sweat that had formed, and opened the door. I walked out onto the porch and waited for Mary to get out of her car. The driver's door opened and her scuffed up cowgirl boots touched the dirt drive. She looked up and caught my eye, and smiled without fear, without trepidation. She walked onto the porch and gave me a warm embrace, not noticing the red cooler or green carpet I had been so worried about. I still had the insecurities of a normal, productive member of society and immediately began to apologize for cabin number three.

"James."
"Yes Mary?"
"Stop it, it's perfect. Show me the inside already." As we walked in, Mary noticed how charming the features in the cabin were, with the cathedral ceiling and farmers porch.

"Do you know what these floors would cost now a days?"
"No clue."
"Wide planked hardwoods are very expensive, James. This place has a lot of charm."

"It has a lot of things, but charm isn't one that comes to mind."
"Well, it's perfect James, and I'm here to spend time with you, not to critique your living arrangements." She walked over to the wicker basket full of albums and flipped through until she found The Best of Coltrane.

"Do you mind?"
"My pleasure Mary," I replied, as I removed the album and placed it on the record player.

"Red or white?" I asked over my shoulder.
"I'm kinda in the mood for red, you?"

"Me too. I was actually hoping you'd say that." By now Mary was sitting at the table and had begun to run her forefinger over the deeply carved letters. She asked about Chico.

"Is he one of your friends?" she asked jokingly.
"No, but I can't tell you how many times I've pondered who he was, and why he stayed here." They both began to theorize on the exploits of the mysterious man known only as Chico.

"He was an international spy during the cold war."
"No way, I've yet to hear of a spy named Chico," laughed Mary.
"Perhaps an old Vietnam vet pilot turned smuggler for a cartel."
"A tree top flyer? I like that one," I replied.
Handing Mary the red wine in a water glass, I apologized for not having proper stemware. Mary informed me that she was quite capable of drinking wine from a bottle, let alone a glass.

"The wine makes the glass, James, not the other way around."
"Thank you, Socrates."
Mary raised her glass and made a toast to the mystery of Chico. "May the intrigue live on forever."

"May every time someone mentions his name, he live another year," I added.

"Oh, I like that one" Mary said as she touched my glass, and shared the first sip of the weekend.

We arrived downtown at half past seven to be certain we would make our eight o'clock reservation. The cold winter air still permeated the near empty harbor. As we made our way down to the wharf, Mary had a difficult time walking on the cobblestones with her black high heels. She reached out and held onto my arm for support, "Thank you cobblestone god" I said loud enough for Mary to hear, and received a smile along with a squeeze on the arm in return.

"Do you know why there are cobblestones in New England Mary?"
"So women have to hold onto the arms of their suitor?"
"Well, that, and they were counterweights for merchant vessels years ago. The ships from Europe needed to be weighted down on the voyage across the ocean. Once they reached the port in New England, they would unload the stones to allow room for grain or whatever. Huge piles of the stone started to build up, so someone came up with the idea of using them for streets."

"Only you would know that, James."

We continued to walk arm and arm past the boutiques and shops until we reached the restaurant directly on the water. I opened the door and gestured for Mary to enter first. We were greeted by the same host I had tipped on the prior day. He approached with a warm welcome as if I was a regular. I went along with the friendly embrace in hopes of impressing Mary.

"Your table is ready sir. Would you like to be seated now or have a drink at the bar?"

I looked at Mary and said, "You're the boss" allowing her to make the decision.

"I would love to sit now, if you don't mind. My feet are killing me from walking on all those counterweights."

The host obliged, and escorted us to the most desirable seat in the house. He pulled out Mary's chair and helped her sit as he told her what a great man she was with. As he walked away, I shook his hand with another twenty-dollar bill. "Thanks for all your help."

"Anytime sir. Enjoy your meal," the host answered, as he winked without Mary's knowledge, and walked back to his stand, undoubtedly to preform the exact same routine for the next paying patron.

"What a beautiful place James," Mary commented, as she looked around and admired the wide planked floors, and black and white etchings of different generals from the Revolutionary war hanging on the walls. The room was as dark as a two hundred year old restaurant ought to be on a cold winter's night, illuminated only by the flames of the burning wood from the fireplace, along with the candles that were set on each table. A few gas lamps on the walls also added to the ambience. An old picture of George Washington crossing the Delaware hung above the fireplace. Below, there was a musket resting on the wooden shelf. The smoky scent of two hundred years worth of fire soaked into the bones.

"Do you like oysters Mary?"
"No.... I love them. I actually lived on Prince Edward Island for a summer back in college. My roommate had a summer home there and I was able to stay with her family. Those are on my short list of favorites."

"I am so glad that you like, I mean love, oysters Mary."
"Why's that?"
"Well, I'm not sure why, but I can't eat oysters alone. It's kind of an intimate experience between two people. It's odd though, because if we ordered calamari for an appetizer, it would be just that, an appetizer. But oysters are a completely different story; there is a certain romance in sharing them. I have no clue why, but it just is."

"I totally agree James. I'm glad you didn't want the calamari." Mary concurred, smiling.

As we locked eyes again, we shared a beautiful silence. Although not a word was spoken, the exchange was far deeper than any intimate dialogue could have captured. Our waiter, who approached the table wearing formal black attire, eventually interrupted the gaze. I ordered a bottle of Cabernet and a dozen Prince Edward Island oysters. The server returned with the oysters and the hot sauce I had requested to save him a trip. He opened the bottle of wine and handed me the cork, which I immediately handed to Mary. This time, instead of laughing at the absurd gesture, Mary held the cork, closed her eyes and inhaled as if she was a professional sommelier. She nodded in acceptance of the wine and preceded to hand the cork back to me, where I repeated the ritual. The waiter poured both glasses and walked away. As soon as he was about ten feet from the table, we both gave in to the overwhelming urge to giggle like a couple of children in church that couldn't control their forbidden laughter.

"You should have gone to Hollywood," I said, acknowledging her performance.

"You were pretty good too James. Honestly, I greatly appreciate you bringing me to this place; it's stunning, and I was able to smell a cork. But you do realize that I would share a box of wine with you right now in front of that fireplace, right?"

"I do Mary; that's why I brought you here. That, and I wanted to let you know how much you mean to me."

"Oh James, you impressed me that first night when I saw how you treated your children and Tex."

"At the risk of sounding corny, I just really like you Mary. I felt a special connection the second you lifted your head from the book you were reading and looked at me. What were you reading anyway?"

"The Picture of Dorian Gray."
"Oscar Wilde, very nice."

I was well aware that I had just committed the cardinal sin of courtships by wearing my heart on my sleeve and telling her my feelings, but I didn't care. I was sick of all the games in the dating world, and wasn't about to play them with Mary. She sensed my vulnerability and, as a sign of reassurance, reached her right hand across the table and gently held my left.

"I'm falling too James, and I'm not wearing a parachute either."
"Falling is the best part, Mary. I'm just not a big fan of the sudden stop at the end; that's what will break you."

"I'll catch you, if you catch me, James."
"Deal." And with my free hand, I raised my crystal stemmed wine glass and made a toast. "To cobblestones and gravity."

"To cobblestones and gravity," Mary repeated.
The waiter returned and our order was placed. Mary ordered steak, rare. I decided on the baked stuffed lobster. There was something sexy about a woman ordering a steak. I didn't ponder why, but noticed the effect and continued with the conversation.

"Those cabins are so cute, James. They remind me of an artist village in Sausalito."

"Cute? Really?"

"Yes, honest."

"I've accepted my living conditions and oddly enough have grown to remotely like them, but I would never describe them as charming or cute."

"Well, not right now they aren't, but if you gave them a little love and a fresh coat of paint, you'd be surprised. The framework is solid. Where else could you find a bunch of little cabins with farmers' porches and cathedral ceilings? The possibilities are endless."

"Really? What possibilities are you talking about that doesn't invovle several sticks of dynamite, because Tex just confided in me this morning that he is going to lose the property after the next tax cycle."

"Oh my God, that's terrible."

"I know, please don't tell him that I told you; he'd kill me."

"No, never, but he seems to warm up to me, so I'll let him tell me this weekend."

"He tries to keep it going, but he makes no money. I mean I've been staying there for a few months now and besides a few afternoon delights, I can't recall anyone else staying the night."

Mary spoke before thinking: "Well, who in their right mind would..." she caught herself and apologized.

"No need, I totally get it. I thought the same thing every time I drove by the place too."

"No, I'm sorry. One should never judge another's situation; I know better."

"All is forgiven. Now tell me about your idea."

"Well, I've always been a local artist at heart and supported others wherever I've lived, be it Key West, California or Cape Cod. I believe that there is a community out there in every town in America that supports local grass roots talent."

"That's great, but what does that have to do with the cabins?"

"The supermarkets, big box stores and pesticides are ruining America and many people are starting to become very aware of the ominous results that will evolve. Those people are buying local. Wouldn't you rather buy your produce or coffee from someone you see around town, rather than having them shipped frozen from God knows where?"

"Of course I would, but I'm kind of lost right now."

"There is no place around here for a community like that to exist James."

"So you want them to live in the cabins?"

"Oh James, bless your heart," Mary replied to tease me about not understanding what she was trying to tell me.

"No, give them a place to sell their goods, kind of like where you met me. Tex could clean out the cabins and rent to local artists to create a village, a destination for people to buy local. Just imagine a few cabins for artists, just like the one I had, maybe one for a blacksmith? One could become a coffee shop, maybe even an oyster bar? The possibilities are endless James."

"He does own the property, so there is no mortgage on it. And I know Tex; he just needs enough money to survive and pay his taxes."

"I think it could work James. I mean he would have to demolish the really bad ones, and fill in that hole in the ground he calls a pool. He'd have to get several dumpsters to remove all the mattresses and things, do some landscaping, and buy a few buckets of paint, but then he's in business."

"That's actually a pretty good idea Mary. I just wonder if Tex would be open to it. I mean, he's a tough as nails war veteran, but he also believes that we are all angels, so your guess is as good as mine."

"Well, it's a sinking ship right now, so maybe he'll be open to it."
"It sounds awesome. I'd love to be a part of something like that. There is no sense of neighborhood anymore. It would be nice to bring a little piece of that back," I added.

The food arrived and was just as delightful as the conversation. I cut the first piece of my shrimp and offered it to Mary. "Open up, first bite."

"It's excellent James," Mary said while covering her mouth with the white linen napkin. "I guess chivalry isn't dead."

"No, I just wanted you to have the first piece in case it was poisoned," I laughingly replied.

"Very fresh James, very fresh."
    I found it both sexy and innocent that Mary used "fresh" to describe my antics. In return, she cut off a small piece off the end of her steak, placed a small chunk of crumbled blue cheese on her fork and raised it. I opened my mouth in anticipation of the morsel but Mary ever so softly lifted her fork and touched the tip of my nose with the steak, and *then* put it in my mouth.
"Oh sorry, my eyes must be going," she said.

"Touche Mary, touche."
After the entrees, we split an order of tiramisu at the insistence of the waiter. It was a completely unnecessary addition because we both were full from dinner, but neither of us wanted the date to end so we ate until we had eaten way too much, plus a double espresso for me and a Cappuccino for Mary.

"I always get mine with skim milk, she said, but what's the use after this meal?"

"I know, I should have put my fork down ten minutes ago," I said.

The bill came and I placed my credit card on top of the black leather folder and handed it to the waiter without looking at the amount.

"James, let me pay half. How much was it?"
"No clue. It probably looks like a phone number though. Buy me breakfast in the morning and we'll call it even."

Mary insisted on paying a portion or at least leaving the tip, but I refused her offer.

"Mary, I asked you here, so it's my treat. It's just refreshing to see a woman make an attempt to pay a bill. I can't tell you how many times I went out on dates and they didn't even reach. I mean, they weren't going to pay anyways, but at least throw a shoulder into it, a head fake, something," I said, smiling at my ridiculousness.

"You're insane, James."
"Totally," I agreed. "But I can't comprehend that women want equal rights, which I completely support, but then they want the man to pay for everything. They can't have it both ways."

"Oddly enough, I agree with you James. You must have dated the wrong girls."

"Well obviously," I smiled at Mary.
As we stood to leave, the host came over and helped Mary with the three quarter length winter jacket that she had

bought at the Salvation Army. He inquired about the meal, to which both gave rave reviews.

"James, you should take your 'stand up' on the road."
I pretended to tighten an imaginary tie and replied with my best, but awful impression of Rodney Dangerfield: "No respect I tell ya, no respect."

"On second thought, don't quit your day job," Mary quipped.
"You look great in that jacket," I told Mary.
"Thanks, it's vintage hounds tooth. I paid thirty dollars for it."
"Really? It looks great."
"Yup, I bought it at the thrift store before the winter. They also sell wine glasses there you know," Mary teased.

"Looks like I'm not the only jokester in this relationship."
"I'm afraid you have met your match James."
"I hope so Mary, I truly do," as smiles equally bright, lit up both faces as we made our way to the exit. A gust of cold, dark winter's air slapped our faces when I opened the door for Mary. I looked up at the cloudless night as I always do when first stepping outside. We strolled arm in arm the twenty yards to reach the water's edge. There we leaned against the thick rope that prevented children from falling into the water during the summer months. Mary was now standing in front of me with both my arms interlocked around her midsection. We both began to stargaze.
"Isn't it crazy that there are billions of stars and planets out there, and we only know a handful?"

"It makes our problems seem very small, doesn't it James? Do you know that the ring around Saturn is made up of millions of little moons and chunks of ice?" Mary added.

"I don't want to toot my own horn, but I did know that. I'm just excited that you don't think I'm nuts for wondering what's out there Mary."

"I think people are ignorant that don't."

After a few minutes of enjoying the vast and ever expanding universe above, the winter chill pierced our polyester and cotton protective barriers, so we decided to walk to the car. Since power locks weren't an option on the Rabbit in nineteen eighty-three, I took her keys out of my jacket pocket and unlocked the passenger door. As I opened it, Mary turned around and passionately kissed me. The first few seconds were awkward as most first kisses are, but as soon as I figured out clockwise or counter clockwise, we eventually found a lovely pattern and continued like a couple of high school kids hiding at the bottom of a stairwell between classes. The drive back to cabin number three was filled with innocent caressing and a few more primal gestures. I opened the front door and offered Mary a glass of the red wine that was already open from before dinner. She answered me with another passionate kiss.

"I guess that's a no."
"Shut up James."
I muffled a "sorry" between kisses.

We quickly unbuttoned each other's clothing and with a few shakes of our hips we allowed gravity do the rest, except for those damn stockings that always cause a five second delay, giving a woman an opportunity to rethink the situation. I removed her dress, but unsuccessfully attempted to remove her bra. After a valiant effort I decided to move on to her underwear. Noticing the difficulty I was having, she removed it herself in less than a second. She unbuckled my belt and opened my pants. I did the rest to speed the process. I gently laid her down on the bed and began to kiss her neck, slowly moving down and around her perfectly natural breasts. From there I made my way to the belly button, where I placed a delicate kiss while she ran her fingers through my hair. I then lightly kissed my way to the final destination of the square root of nature: "Pie." I was faced with the most intricate and beautiful creation of all mankind. Just as in my dance moves, I outlined the letters of the alphabet, ever so gently at first, until she moaned, pleading for more. She spread her legs, writhing with eager anticipation. My objective of bringing her to delightful orgasm was easily achieved. After climaxing, she grabbed me under my arms and pulled me up so that our reproductive organs were aligned perfectly like the heavens above. I guided my hard penis, sliding it into her already soaking wet vagina. Its swollen soft sides encased me. I started out slowly, moving my hips back and forth while kissing her softly on the mouth until the gentle love making naturally progressed into more aggressive animalistic antics. About twenty minutes into the growing ecstasy of exploring various sexual positions and arousal pleasures, I could hold it no longer, and exploded in orgasm into Mary's still thrusting hips. This triggered Mary to have a second even more powerful one. I collapsed on top of her chest in complete satisfaction. After I lay motionless for a few minutes, Mary informed me that I was killing her.

"Oh sorry" I said, immediately rolling off, to lie by her side.

I placed Mary's hand over my pounding heart so she could feel each beat as if it was going to break through my chest. Not a word was spoken; it had all been said. We fell asleep spooning, I the little and Mary the big.

I woke before Mary, carefully removed my numb arm from underneath her neck, and walked over to the counter-top to make my customary pot of imported coffee. Still naked from the night's activities, I turned around and watched Mary sleep for several seconds, just long enough to witness her chest moving from the mechanics of breathing. I sat at Chico's table and immediately felt the cold wood from the chair on my unprotected testicles. I began to thumb through a local magazine that I'd picked up for free while exiting the market. "Mary was right," I thought looking through several advertisements for various local artists, each located in a different place. How great would it be if Tex could provide one central location for them; everyone could feed off of the whole crowd of people strolling around. It could be perfect I thought. I assumed that most artists struggle and couldn't afford rent in a stand-alone location, and also knew that all Tex wanted was enough money to survive and pay his bills. One of his famous quotes with me was "Pigs get fed, hogs get slaughtered, so don't ever become a hog, kid." Add to that the fact that Tex might be able to bring a small piece of Americana back to the State, and chills would be sent up his spine.

Mary started to wake from the absence of body heat and aroma of freshly brewed coffee, or perhaps it was the soft cry of "Holy shit" when I had landed on the cold chair. She sat up on her elbows and looked at me and unlike in the movies, there was no perfectly placed bed sheet covering her breasts. I stood up and walked the three feet to the counter and poured us each a cup of coffee, Mary's first. She stared at my ass, as I did her exposed breasts, both very pleased with what we saw. She sat on the edge of the bed, using it as a chair at Chico's table. There we discussed, still comfortably nude, the possibilities of Mary's idea while I showed her the magazine.

"Let's get dressed and tell Tex your Idea, Mary."
"Sounds good, but before we do, get your sexy behind back in bed."

I didn't hesitate to fulfill Mary's request of making morning love, sans the foreplay. We both were conscience of not having brushed our teeth, but a little less kissing did not diminish the mutual pleasure. After our first delightful morning sex session, I stood to walk into the shower. "I'd ask you to join me Mary, but the shower is about the size of a coffin. I'll be right out, just need to rinse off."

Mary laughed and remained in bed while I corrected the water temperature and got in. She couldn't help but think of the irony, that when she was married she had a shower big enough for five people but never wanted to join as a pair. Now she found herself getting out of bed and cramming herself in the shower with me. "Square footage doesn't equate to love," she thought to herself for the first time.

Finally fully clothed, we drove into town discussing the options for breakfast. Mary wanted to eat healthy; I just wanted to eat. I came to the realization that even though I'd lived here my whole life, I really never walked around to learn the history of my own town. There were several museums that I had stumbled past as a college kid but the thought of entering never crossed my mind. Today I was sober and interested in seeing Rembrandt, so I became a tourist in my hometown. "I bring luck where ever I go, James," Mary said, as we found a much-coveted parking space on Main Street. We walked past a row of clapboard houses each with an historic sign signifying the sea Captain or Revolutionary War hero who resided there years ago. Across the street I saw a sign that simply said "EAT" glowing in the window. "Let's see if they serve breakfast," I said. And as Mary's luck would have it, they did. We waited for a few minutes, but were seated in a timely fashion by the owner, who wasn't too proud to clear tables and seat people.

We ordered the same thing off the menu, egg white omelets with steamed spinach. I gladly accepted the home fries while Mary opted for the fruit cup. The discussion revolved around the cabins and what would have to be done in order to accomplish the mission - zoning boards, insurance policies, construction costs, and the like. I told Mary that my ex brother-in-law worked for the zoning commission and thought that he would lend a helping hand. He was always super nice to me because he knew that his sister was difficult, to say the least. Even though I wanted to, I never spoke ill of my cheating, empty, insecure, toxic, and diabolical ex.

After breakfast, Mary and I decided to wander though downtown, past all the docks, shops and museums. We stopped at several and eventually purchased a braided necklace for Mary. The stroll was perforated with a glass of wine or two along with the sharing of a slice of apple pie. I decided to call Tex and fill him in on the discussion. As soon as he answered, I handed the phone to Mary.

"Hello?"
"Is the most handsome man in America there?"
"I'm not sure I'm the best looking guy in America, but I am certainly better looking than the guy standing next to you," Tex replied.

After a few pleasantries, Mary asked Tex if he would like to join us for dinner, to which he politely declined. "You kids enjoy yourselves, I'm fine."

"Nonsense Walter, we will pick you up in thirty minutes and you best look sharp."

"I could wear a potato sack, and look like a million bucks."

"I'm sure you could. We'll see you then, good bye." She handed the phone back to me.

I said hello, but Tex had already hung up. "What did he say?"

"We need to pick him up. He's coming."

Thirty minutes later we pulled into the cabins. Tex was standing there in a light blue and white-checkered button down shirt, with the sleeves rolled up past his elbows, exposing his faded tattoo and infantry watch. The shirt was tucked neatly into a pair of dark blue jeans. He glanced at his watch and gave us a look of approval for our timeliness. Mary exited, opened the rear door and sat in the backseat of her own car. Tex adamantly refused, but Mary was insistent that he sit in the front seat. He didn't argue further but mumbled something in reference to Mary as he entered.

We sat down and ordered the pizza the only way red-blooded Americans should: large, cheese and with pepperoni. Prior to the pizza's arrival, but only after the first mouthful of draft beer, did I work up the courage to begin telling Tex about Mary's idea.

"Mary came up with a plan that might save the cottages, but you have to think outside the box."

Tex just looked at me blankly for a long second and replied, "I'm all ears."

In her naturally calming voice, Mary said "Tex, you have to remove yourself from your comfort zone for a moment, and be open to a suggestion."

"Ok darling, I promise." Tex replied.
"An artist village."
"An artist who?"
"An artist village, Tex" I said. Just hear Mary out. You said you are going to lose the place after the next tax cycle anyways, so what's the downside?

Mary continued, "Tex, you obviously have trouble renting the cottages, correct?"

"Occupancy has been slow."
"To put it politely," I interjected.
"James showed me around this afternoon and showed me how beautiful this town is. There are expensive hotels and condos popping up everywhere, with indoor pools, saunas, Jacuzzis, spas and tennis courts, you name it, they have it. You can't compete with those, Tex."

"Tell me something I don't know."
"Well, on top of all those things I just pointed out, the cabins are in need of a lot of love too."

"Love?" I questioned. "Yeah, that and a bulldozer."
"Very funny. You two are going to give me more agita than the pepperoni!"

Mary asked Tex how many cabins were on the property, to which Tex replied "twentyish."

"Twentyish? Shouldn't that be an absolute number there, Cowboy?"
"Yes, it should be, but I don't know if you want to count the two that have collapsed roofs."

"Yeah, no, we don't need to count those."
"Ok, eighteen cabins then."
"Perfect, and how many are in need of demolition?
"I don't think any. Maybe one would need to be addressed," Tex said, with a dose of denial evident in his response.

Mary accepted his mischaracterization of the truth and moved on without comment. "Ok, so we will pick the best fifteen and remove the worst three units. The others we can save with a little bit of sweat equity, paint, and . . . love," she finished after a pause to turn her head towards me."

I chimed in, "We'll need to get a few dumpsters and rent a bulldozer, gut everything - the beds, tables, countertops, everything. We need to fix all the rotted wood and repaint each one, and obviously replace all the broken windows."

"Each could be a place for selling unique goods, maybe two vendors in some cabins to help the farmers/bakers/artists with the costs, maybe a coffee shop in one, so many other possibilities Tex. Imagine all the tourists coming to the cabins and walking around like you guys did on the Cape, but your place would be so much better Tex, you have to believe me." Mary promised.

"We three could start the renovations to save on labor costs. I'll market the hell out of it to those cookie cutter resorts that you hate," I said to Tex.

"Tex replied, "Sometimes you have to dance with the devil."
"So does that mean you like it?"
"What the hell do I know about running an artist village?"
Dinner came and all three fell silent as we enjoyed their pizza – complete with the legitimate kind of circular pepperoni that curls up creating a pool of grease in the middle. I noticed that Mary didn't soak hers up with her napkin. "She's definitely a keeper." I thought to myself. After the second slice and third beer, I asked Tex his thoughts.

Tex inhaled and held his breath for several seconds, as if he was smoking an imaginary cigarette, similar to the ones he gave up after the war on insistence from his wife. A few seconds past, after which he said, "I love it, I really love it."

"You do?" I exclaimed.
"Yes, I have no idea how we will get it done, but I love it," Tex repeated, as he raised his beer for a toast. "Here's to those who wish us well, all the rest can go to hell."

At that, all three rims touched each other's harder than anticipated, causing some of the contents from each glass to spill on the pizza.

"That's alright, the grease will soak it up, laughed Mary."

After we were finished, the waitress cleared the empty pizza tray, along with all the paper plates and napkins that were stained different shades of orange.
"Another round of beers please, doll." Tex said, as he began to write down his finances on a clean napkin, while Mary was busy writing several different names of artists she could contact.

"I wonder if this is how all businesses start," I wondered allowed.
"Well, tell me one successful business that was discussed over a salad," challenged Tex.

"We need to go see the vultures at City Hall and apply for a variance. I'm sure they'll deny it because it might actually be good for the community." Tex griped.

"It's all set," I assured him. "I already called my brother-in-law and he assured me that it will pass, I told him that we wanted to showcase some local high school talent, and he ate it up."

"You're a genius kid."

"Why thank you, grandpa."
"This grandpa will still kick your ass, sonny boy."
"Now boys," Mary said to interject a nugget. "May I share a quote from Mark Twain?"

"Of course you can." Tex replied.
"The two most important days in your life are the day you are born, and the day you find out why."

"Wow, that's pretty deep Mary," I said as I smiled at the realization that Mary was so connected to the universe.
"Maybe we all just found out the why."
"We finished up the conversation along with our beers by figuring out what Tex needed to charge for rent in order for it to be successful, and for him to survive. Mary suggested seven hundred dollars a month for each cabin.

"Nonsense" Tex replied. "I don't need that much money to live; five hundred per cabin is enough money for me to make ends meet."

"You are such a good man, Tex", Mary said.
"The jury is still out on that one," I chimed in.
"I think you know where you can put this glass of beer," Tex answered.
"Procrastination is the enemy of forward progress, and nothing can survive in stagnation." Tex had told me too many times to count.

The only thing that can cause results, is action, so the following morning over coffee and Elvis, we immediately began to create a blue print for success. I took Tex to visit my ex brother-in-law at city hall to help navigate the zoning process, or as Tex put it, "Horse shit wrapped in red tape." The brother-in-law made sure that Tex filled out the proper documentation and delivered the paperwork to the right people. Tex realized that he was an asset, but at the same time it bothered him that this was the only way to get things done at City hall. Mary stayed in cabin number three, and worked on the logistics at Chico's table. When we returned to my cabin, we were greeted with an incredible rendering of the new artist village. It was a black and white pencil drawing, complete with crisp lines and people walking around the fifteen remaining cabins, along with a gazebo in the courtyard where the empty pool currently resided.

"You're quite the artist, Mary."
"Thanks handsome," she replied to Tex.
"But now for the piece de resistance, are you two ready?"
"Yes ma'am, what do you have?" I asked.
"I came up with a name!" Mary exclaimed, unable to control her excitement.
"What is it?" asked Tex. "Here me out. It's a place where people will sell local goods and art, a place where local bands will play, maybe sell local produce, and Tex always talks about how one needs forward progress everyday, right?"

"Pretty much." Tex said.

"Ok, so here it is." Mary said, as she turned over a piece of paper to reveal a cursive drawing of *Local motion*. "What do you think?"

"Local Motion" Tex replied straight faced as a professional poker player holding a shitty hand.

"Get it? It's all about local, and we are in forward motion."
"I like it," said Tex.
"I love it too, I think it's great," I encouraged, perhaps a tad biased. "Actually, it kinda looks like a train with all the cabins in a row," I added.

Mary had to leave after the unveiling of her masterpiece so, while we were at city hall, she had packed her overnight bag, and left a note under my pillow only to be found after she left. She thanked me for a wonderful weekend and gave me a loving embrace with a kiss on the lips. She then gave Tex the same hug, sans the kiss on the lips, instead resorting to his weathered cheek. We each thanked her for all that she did, and her great idea.

"Au revoir" Mary said.
"Make sure you call me when you get home, so I know you got there safe." I called out.

"Will do." She walked away without turning back, but just as she was getting into her light blue VW Rabbit, she turned around and blew me a kiss. "Until we meet again."

"Hey!" Tex yelled from across the small farmers porch.
Mary leaned her head out the already opened drivers side
window. "Yes dear?
"Knock, knock."
"Who's there?"
"The old man who doesn't like the name."
"The old man who doesn't like the name, who?"
"The old man who friggin loves the name, that's who."
Mary just smiled as she felt the long lost felling of pride and
self-worth slowing returning to her soul, a feeling her ex hus-
band stole from her over the years due to his own insecurities.

CHAPTER 13

———— ⚜ ————

Local Motion

THE FOLLOWING WEEKS were divergent than the meaningless ones of the past. Tex was not just existing on this planet anymore; he was now living, and living with a purpose. One morning, I awoke to the distinct sound of forged steel striking a solid object. I opened my door, and walked out to see Tex swinging a hammer against the rusted hinges of a door jam to make room for the removal of the mattress and countertops. I then noticed that a dumpster had magically appeared sometime during the night.

"What are you doing old timer?" I said as I valiantly picked at the crust that formed in the corner of my eye during the night.
"What does it look like I'm doing, Alice? Now come help me get this frame off."

"The Zoning Board hasn't even conducted the hearing yet; do you think we should be doing this?"

"Better to beg for forgiveness, than to ask for permission," Tex replied.

"True." I said as I began to walk over and help remove those damn ugly, brown, stubborn screws that somehow melted into the doorframe.

"We need to get this done today because my friend is letting me borrow his back hoe tomorrow; we need to get all this crap into the dumpster before we knock this one down. I hope you brought your A game kid."

"Always do, grandpa."
"I'm knocking this one down along with those two over there," Tex said as he pointed with his already bleeding right arm. Tex and I worked like bulls all day, only stopping every so often for a beer and a quick bite to eat. I marveled at how much work an old man, and a guy who only performed manual labor by mistake had accomplished. By the end of the long day, we were covered in sweat and dirt. Somehow the pants Tex was wearing had several spots of blood, though he never found the source. I walked onto the porch of cabin number three and retrieved two long neck green bottles of beer from the red cooler.

"Do you think Mary knows what she's talking about?"
"Honestly Tex, I do. I have a great feeling about this. There is risk in everything we do, but this is a calculated one."

"I guess you're right, kid." Tex replied.
"What else were you going to do with this place anyways?"
"Well, probably burn it for insurance money."
"Ha. Good one."

"What?" Tex said absent a smile.

The next morning came way too early, as it tends to do after an honest day of hard work. Each woke up in separate cabins but bitched about the same stiffness in our lower backs. "God damn it," said Tex. "Jesus Christ!" I complained. The backhoe was dropped off at seven o'clock sharp as promised, Tex didn't waste any time; at three past the hour, he drove it straight towards the cabin. I stood back and marveled at how proficient Tex was at operating such a machine. Within ten minutes the cabin was all but completely leveled. Tex then parked the backhoe next to the debris and lowered the large bucket so we could begin to fill it. After we painstakingly filled the bucket with debris, Tex discarded the load into the dumpster. By the end of the day, three dumpsters were full and all that was left of the three cabins was a cement slab – its former foundation. Tex made quick work out of slamming the bottom of the bucket to break it into small sections, then burying it. Everything went as planned, except when Tex allowed me to drive the backhoe through the last cabin. I didn't strike the corner as hard as Tex had instructed, which caused the backhoe to become wedged between the walls. After a few minutes, I managed to wiggle my way out, and demolished the cabin with the brute force of modern day machinery, I yelled over the roar of the diesel engine. "Wahoo!" "All those sessions with my shrink, and yoga classes have nothing on this." As I thought to myself that there must be a primal instinct in each of us, when it comes to the exhilaration destruction provides us.

The next weekend was my turn for visitation, and unlike the previous visits, I decided to bring the girls to the cabin. All the anxiety and guilt I had felt for not being able to provide my children with the finer things were all for naut. Those feelings were impostors - liars to my soul. The minute the girls jumped out of my car, they began to run though the courtyard and into a few cabins. They likened each to a tree house without the tree. "It's just like a fort daddy, it's so cool!" yelled the little one. I then came to the realization that children have no concept of being poor, or whether or not the house that they live in is small, or the car that brings them to school has high millage. All they care about is love, and cupcakes; they care about cupcakes.

"Get over here and give your dad a hug." While we were embraced in a three-person hug, I started to wipe the tears from my eyes.

"Daddy, not again," my oldest said in a loving voice.

"Oh sorry puddin' pie. I just love you girls so much, and you make me so proud. Now who wants to help daddy and Tex paint?"

"I do, I do!" the girls yelled, as if I had offered to buy them ice cream.

We changed into old clothes and walked over to the cabin that Tex had already begun to paint.

"We have a few helpers today, boss."

"Hey kids, how are you? Tex asked, as he gave them an armless embrace due to the paint all over his hands. "Will you ladies accept one dollar an hour for your help?"

Both girls accepted Tex's monetary offer and began to paint. I joked that there was some child labor law being broken, to which Tex replied. "Yeah, and tax evasion too."
Knowing better than to give my littlest one paint, I filled a small bucket with water and handed her a small brush. She began to paint water on a section of wall and couldn't have been happier. Tex had replaced most of the rotted wood on the unit and removed all the old carpet unveiling a modest masterpiece.

"I can't believe that you're not keeping the miniature golf turf on the porches. That was such a nice touch I said, knowing that I had diplomatic immunity from Tex's sharp tongue, due to the presence of children. Tex just looked at me and said, "I think you know what you can do with that comment."

I couldn't let up: "No honestly, I just heard that the resort being built across the street just ordered a few rolls of it, to put on their decks."
Tex suddenly had an itch on the middle of his forehead just above his nose, and decided to scratch using his middle finger. Tex had learned in boot camp that there are several ways to tell someone to go fuck themselves, without having to say "go fuck yourself." Scratching his forehead with his middle finger fit this occasion.

Tex had decided on the simplistic look of white paint. We painted both the interior and exterior of one cabin that day, with key support from my laptop and several DVD's of various princess cartoons, to occupy the girls after the painting had lost it's zest. Tex still paid them ten dollars each and promised them junk food later that night.

"One down, and about a dozen to go," he commented.
"Don't remind me," I replied, while noting how much bigger the cabins appeared now that they were void of furniture.

The weekend came and went with lightening fast speed, as it always did when I had my girls. They were so excited to come back to the cabins and play hide and seek. In reality they played in a small, freshly painted cabin, but in their minds it was a castle in some far away European countryside surrounded by a moat. Other times it was a pirate ship, with the burnt sporadic grass being the ocean filled with sharks and mermaids. No matter what was reality to us adults, it was a magical world to children. It made me think of that lonely walk from the courthouse when I came to the conclusion that everyone has a different universe. The universe of a child is completely different than the universe of the parent. In a child's' universe, stuffed animals come to life and fairies leave a dollar under the pillow in exchange for a tooth. In the same house, but in a different universe, the parents worry about bills and the opinions of insignificant people. The universe of a Wall Street executive is different than that of the homeless man he pretends he doesn't see each morning as he walks by. I'm still wondering which universe was best to call home.

That week Tex and I attended the zoning board hearing at which we watched our project get rubber-stamped. The Board asked several standard questions, which we answered freely, without the advice of counsel. Tex decided to allow me to explain the business model. I showed the rendering that Mary designed, and explained my desire to have local high school children showcase their art. The only concern they had was the fact that Tex had applied for a liquor and entertainment license, but the matter was quickly resolved with an agreement between Tex and the Board. They agreed that there would only be local bands and the alcohol and music would end at ten pm. The meeting adjourned and both sides thanked each other for their time. As I was exiting the room, I saw my brother-in-law and ever so slightly, nodded my head in appreciation and as not to expose a friendship. The brother-in-law still feeling guilty for how his sister had harpooned me, nodded back with a smile.

On the way home we visited the headquarters of two local publications, the kind that are given away free at every coffee shop and supermarket in town. After placing an advertisement, we drove straight to an oyster farm on the edge of town and spoke to the owner, harvester, boat captain, and CEO - all of which were embodied in the same person, Jimmy.

"Tex, you old bastard, what are you doing here?"
"Nothing, I felt like getting food poisoning, so I figured I'd stop by."

After the embrace of two old friends who hadn't seen each other in much too long, I explained the concept of Local Motion to Jimmy. He was very interested, and planned on visiting the site within the next few days.

While we were driving back home, I surprised Tex by saying, "I want one."

"Want one what?" he asked.

"A cabin, I want a cabin."

"For what?"

"You know I've always wanted to open a coffee shop. Well, I was always too nervous to take the chance; I've always let the fear of failure hold me back. That, and the fact that I didn't have a hundred grand for the build out."

"You have always talked about that damn coffee shop of yours," Tex replied.

"I kinda want to be involved in this project."

"You are involved kid. Without you, none of this would be happening."

"You saved me Tex. I want one. I'm taking a shot; I don't want to be one of those people that look back on their life and ask, "What could have been?"

"Don't ever let the fear of failure hold you back, kid. Pick whichever one you want, I don't care. And we will do the build out; it won't cost anything."

"Well, the espresso machine alone is about five grand."
"What?"
"Yup, that's what they go for, and I definitely need one."
"Well, if you are going to do it, do it right. Don't rush to failure. Tex then told him the story of how when he was in the military, he had rushed to help his buddies and left his gun behind. "Imagine, running right into a world of shit to help my brothers in arms, and leaving my weapon behind." But that taught me a valuable lesson; don't ever rush to failure."

"I know it sounds corny, but it's always been my dream to wake up early, unlock the door of a coffee shop, turn the machines on, chit chat with the customers and live a happy life."

Sounds great Hemingway. "It's not always about money; it's about following your dreams and being happy," Tex concurred.

"Very true, but money doesn't hurt. Have you ever seen someone unhappy on a boat?"

"Good point kid, but do you know what's better than owning a boat?"
"What?"
"Having a best friend that owns a boat."
"Good one," I replied. "You don't care which one I take?"

"Not at all kid. I don't think you know how much you mean to me."

"I do Tex, and the same goes for you."

Tex cut me off in mid sentence, "Alright, alright, which one you want?"

"I think the end unit would be best because I could widen the farmers' porch on the far side to fit more tables."

"That's a great idea. We could build it in a day, Tex said. "Might cost a grand in wood."

A few days later Jimmy called Tex to come down and check out the project. "Don't forget the coffees, kid,"

"How you drink it old man?" Jimmy inquired.

"Black, like my soul."

"No other way to have it. Give me twenty minutes."

"I'll be here painting. Take your time."

Jimmy showed up holding two cups of coffee and handed one to Tex. They walked around the property and entered the three units that were complete. Jimmy saw the potential and loved the idea of an artist village across the street from the largest construction site in the Tri-state area.

"I can't believe old man Anderson sold that farm. How many units are going in there anyway?"

"No clue. Too many if you ask me," Tex replied.

"Nonsense Tex. All those jerks in the Range Rovers and Bentleys that are buying them will spend their money here. It gives them something to do between the country club and fundraisers."

"True. I have always looked at them as a nuisance but I guess I need to change my perspective," Tex acknowledged.

"Absolutely, they feel guilty about being rich and love to think of themselves as common folk, so they will come here and hopefully buy some art, oysters and coffee."

"I'll take a cabin."
"Really?"
"Yes, it will be perfect. I'll only have a few stools in the front of the oyster bar, a couple of high top tables right here and one table on each side of the deck. It's perfect."

"Great, thanks so much, I'm excited to have you Jim." Hemingway is putting a coffee shop in that one right there," Tex said as he pointed to the end unit.

"Great, I'll be his first customer every morning. Is there any truth to the rumor that Oprah bought the penthouse across the street?"

"That's what I heard."

"Look at you, movin' on up. Make sure you tell the kid that he can pick my brain anytime." Jimmy added.

"That mean's a lot, Jim, I'm sure he'll appreciate that very much. This is his first shot at opening a business and he's nervous as hell."

"Tell him that being nervous is a good thing. I was scared to death when I first started my business.

Before Jimmy had become an oyster farmer, he was a good and honest man in an industry that didn't appreciate those attributes. He was the only black man in an office of about seventy people and never felt at home, even though his fellow coworkers were always very polite and invited him to office gatherings, and he was never on the receiving end of direct racial prejudice, he always felt that he had been hired as a token. And a token he was not; he was a very intelligent man. In that office, however, he was marginalized - never given the chance to excel. There were several incidences where someone with less experience was promoted over him and he felt slighted. He could never prove that it was due to his skin color, but he didn't want to wait and work there any longer to find out. So one day he decided to trade in his suit and tie, along with his BMW, for a pair of overalls, a beat up pick-up truck, and a used fourteen foot Boston Whaler.

"I had no clue how to run a business, but my grandfather had always instilled the values of hard work and discipline in me. He would always tell me, "You learn by doin'.""

"Ain't that the truth Jim," Tex said, as he raised his coffee cup and made a toast.

"Here's to a couple of old men."

"To us," Jimmy replied. "Would have been better if it was whiskey."

"Well, bring some next time, you cheap bastard," Tex chided. "You'll never change will you?"

"Nope," Tex replied, as he smiled revealing his crow's feet and gunmetal blue eyes.

"That's why I love ya, pal."

Tex and I soon came to the conclusion that Jimmy was going to make a great addition to the energy at Local Motion. Jimmy chose the cabin exactly in the middle and wasted no time starting with his build out. He somehow located an old barn that was being torn down in a small town in Vermont, drove up there in his pick-up, and loaded the rusty bed with as much reclaimed wood as he could fit. As he pulled up to the cabins, Tex yelled out, "Holy shit Jimmy, How did you manage to get back here without getting pulled over?"

"I didn't," Jimmy yelled back out his driver's side window. As he got out of the truck he explained that the police officer ended up being a great guy who loved oysters. "I told him what we were doing and he thought it was great. I guess he vacations here for a week every summer, so I promised him a couple on the house and he let me go with a warning, adding that the meal would be on him, not the house."

I called back, "Discretion is the better part of valor." Wasting no time, Jimmy began to unload the wood.

I couldn't believe how much interest had evolved so quickly in Local Motion. Artists from all over New England were emailing and calling to learn more about the project. Mary came down more often now to help out and spend time with me. She continued to put her artistic abilities to good use throughout the design and construction periods. She hand painted a unique welcome sign to be hung over each cabin's door.

When the prospective artists showed up and inquired about the property, either Mary or I would show them around and answer any questions they posed. None were aware that not only were they there to ask questions, but that we were interviewing them to ascertain whether or not they would be a good fit in the community. One woman pulled up in her hundred thousand dollar SUV and exited with a dog about the size of a jumbo shrimp in the palm of her hand. She didn't ask - but rather instructed - Tex to show her one of the units. He placed the paintbrush carefully on the edge of the paint can and walked over to introduce himself.

"Hello ma'am, I'm Tex," he said, reaching out to shake her hand, knowing that there was still wet paint on a few of his fingers.

"Uh, hello."

"What a beautiful dog; is it part squirrel?"

"No, this dog was very expensive, I'll have you know."

"I'm sure it was, mean while kids are starving in Africa," Tex mumbled under his breath.

He showed her around a few of the units and, between her cell phone conversations about her tennis lessons, he explained to her the concept of Local Motion.

"I'm moving into the condos across the street and want to open a pocket book boutique. Do you have any bigger units or is this it?"

"You're looking at it, honey. Pocket books you say?"

"Yes, I fly to Europe all the time, and I'm going to import all the top designers' handbags."

"Really?" Tex said, puzzled at the fact that someone would fly to Europe for a purse.

"Well, I'm sorry but all the units are rented, plus, this is for local artists, and I think your idea is different than the model we are going for."

"Too bad I guess, your loss," she said, as she walked back to her SUV."

"Sure is Ma'am, have a wonderful day." Don't forget to pick up a corncob pipe for your husband, he said to himself as he walked back to the cabin he was painting.

The interest in Local Motion exceeded all hopes. Mary, Tex and I were able to sit down and review each artist's portfolio to personally ensure that our village would present itself as a cohesive unit. All the leases were signed and dated to begin for the weekend of Memorial Day. Mary had kept her promise by moving to Rhode Island and leased a cabin. Tex had offered several times but Mary had refused any type of discount on the rent. She packed her belongings into the Volkswagen Rabbit and drove to the Rhode Island coast. On her way she stopped at an antique shop in the town of Chatham. There she bought a five-foot taxidermied marlin for Hemingway's coffee shop. "Lucky you have a sun roof," said the old merchant who helped her place it through the opening. As she drove away, he cupped his hands and yelled, "Good luck with your new adventure!" grinning at the sight of a giant fish head sticking out from the car's sunroof.

Once in Rhode Island, Mary found a beautiful one-room studio loft in a carriage house on the grounds of a beautiful Victorian home built in the 1890's. She wanted to be close enough to James, but far enough away to let him breathe.The place met all of her requirements; it came with a roof, toilet, and a deck big enough for a small bistro set and a grill. Mary not only preached that square footage doesn't equate to the extent of happiness, but she lived it. She particularly appreciated the deck, not because of its size, but due to the fact that if she leaned over the rail on the left, she could see the Atlantic ocean, the same majestic ocean from which she could hear the gentle rhythmic splash of waves on any given night that she left the doors to the deck open. Mary furnished her room by visiting the thrift shops in town. Having been granted permission to do so, she painted the walls a very light pink, and left the trim white, brightening it with a new coat of high gloss paint. She placed a candy apple red, shag rug in the corner of the large room to create a sitting area, so she could enjoy her morning tea and the latest novel, one that usually included a broken heart in the storyline. She found an old Victrola in working condition and bought it "for a song." Although her record collection wasn't nearly as diverse as Hemingway's, it would do for now. She wrapped the Marlin as well as possible and hid it in on the far side of the bed. The older woman who lived in the main house was wonderful, and offered Mary furniture that was stored in the old horse barn. The woman's antique furniture from her grandmother's estate included a cherry wood bed frame and an ornate Chesterfield from the eighteen hundreds. Mary assured her that she would take very good care of them. She also found a beautiful set of Chippendale mahogany chairs. Her gracious landlord told Mary a tale that when George Washington visited with the Governor of the State, he had sat in one of the chairs and discussed the newly formed government. The woman couldn't confirm the story but her grandmother, known to be a God fearing, honest woman, had sworn to its veracity. The lovely lady visited Mary one morning carrying an antique tea set with freshly brewed morning tea. They sat and enjoyed a great conversation during which Mary learned of the woman's late husband and his humble beginning as a watchmaker in Switzerland. When she stood to leave, the woman left the tea set on the antique table that was situated between the Chippendales. Mary stood and attempted to give it back, but the woman insisted that Mary have it, informing her that it had been sitting in the China cabinet since "God knows when" and that it had taken her twenty minutes to clean it.

"Beautiful things weren't meant to sit on shelves Mary, everything needs to live." Mary thanked her profusely, and warmly invited her to come to Tea any time.

CHAPTER 14

More than a Village

BACK AT THE cottages, all the artists were busy preparing for the Grand Opening that was approaching much too soon. The local high school teacher came down and met with Tex and I, to discuss the arrangement for his students to showcase their talents. Tex followed through on his promise and saved half of a cabin's space for the students. The other half was for people in the local hospital that wanted to display their art. The teacher and Tex agreed to having the students clean the property each week in lieu of rent, which entailed cutting the grass, picking weeds, and making sure that the garbage was picked up. Tex was well aware that he was getting the short end of the stick, but his excitement to become an important part of the community was far more important. Throughout his life he had always been guided by a moral compass; it always pointed true North and today was no exception. His principles never wavered.

Tex never thought of Newton's third law, "For every action, there is an equal or greater reaction," when he decided to let students showcase their art for free. The local press picked up on the story and wanted to interview the old war veteran making such an impact on the community. The local paper ran an article on the front page - above the fold - featuring a story along with a picture of Tex talking about the creation of Local Motion. Tex, being the humble man that he is, downplayed his role and highlighted Mary, myself, and all the artists that now called Local Motion their home. The article displayed several pictures of the cabins in various stages of transformation. One photograph was of me preparing an espresso with a large Marlin hanging in the background. Another was of Jimmy sitting on one of the four barstools at the newly named "Toucans' Oyster House." When the reporter asked why he had named it Toucans, Jimmy simply answered, "Because you can only fit two cans of beer on the bar at a time." The article told the whole story of Local Motion, and how it was designed to create a love affair with the community. The writer ended the article by saying that everyone has a story; this one just happens to be incredible.

One of the bad habits of time, is that it travels much too quickly with never a good enough reason to stop. There were only two weeks left until the grand opening of Local Motion and the next chapter of their lives. Mary and I were becoming as one. She spent most nights wearing my XL white, V-neck tee shirt to bed and being the little spoon in my full sized bed. Once in a while we would spend the night at her place, to check on the owner, Evelyn. One early morning at the cabin we heard the usual knock at the door, there stood Tex with a gift wrapped with duct tape and newspaper.

"Come in handsome," Mary said, wearing my white shirt and flannel bottoms she had just put on. I was already up, in the middle of preparing my usual concoction. Tex handed me a gift that I could easily tell was an album, and thanked me for everything I had done. I tore open last week's newspaper, and revealed an unopened Leon Redbone album from 1975.

"Thanks Tex! How did you find this?"
"I had help from Mary; I guess you can find anything on that interweb."
"Internet dear, internet," Mary said, lovingly.
"Whatever it is, it's still scary."
"Don't get him started," I interjected.
I handed Mary the album so she could open it and play side A.

"I love "Ain't Misbehaving," such a great song," I said. We all walked onto the freshly painted porch and enjoyed our morning coffee and some music. The energy was different around the cabins for all to feel. Mary looked at the welcome sign she had painted. Tex was just proud of the whole process, and I was nervously anticipating the opening of my coffee shop. I decided to keep my day job for the benefits, but had cut back my hours and became a part time employee. I planned to open the shop on Friday, Saturday and Sundays at first, to gauge if I could sustain a living or not, but I promised Tex and Mary, that if it became successful, I would resign from my job.

Memorial Day weekend came with a glorious sunrise and mild trepidation of what was to come. Tex had only been able to sleep for a few hours due to his excitement. He rose while the warm blackness of a late May's morning still filled the air. His first order of business was not knocking on my door for a cup of coffee, but the raising of the American flag, on the newly landscaped lawn that was once home to a concrete shell of a pool. Tex had asked all of the tenants to be there at nine am in order to give some opening remarks and introduce everyone. Tex realized that everyone was just as excited as he was, due to the fact that they showed up well before the time he had requested. His objective was to make sure that everyone knew each other before the opening, but it was clearly an unnecessary step because it was readily apparent that everyone already met. At nine am sharp, Tex stood on a picnic table and made a riveting speech about life and the beautiful oddness of it all. He then introduced each person by name, without the need of cue cards, and stated what they did. After each story, there was a round of applause, and a quick word or two by the artist he had introduced. Before he ended, he called up Mary and I to stand next to him on the table, and informed the crowd of what they already knew, but Tex still felt obligated to say. He let everyone know that just a few short months ago he was alone in the world and didn't have a soul to count on. Now he had the biggest family in the State. As he thanked everyone for saving his life, I noticed a tear form in the corner of his eye. It traveled the canals of his crow's feet only to disappear before it reached his chin.

"Thanks again for rescuing this old man," he said while stepping down from the table with the grace of a twenty year old athlete.

Suddenly, and without any warning, a whistle as loud as a train crossing a paved intersection pierced the air. Everyone turned around to identify the source; there Jimmy stood with coffee cup in hand to give an impromptu speech:

"Tex, I think you're the one that did the rescuing. Sometimes the tables of life are tilted - the dice of our existence are loaded and you Tex, you made it a little more fair for all of us. I know I speak for everyone here when I say, we all thank you!"

All the artists began to clap and cheer as if Tex had just hit a grand slam to win the game.

Local motion officially opened at ten am, signified by a couple of vote-seeking politicians cutting a ceremonial ribbon with a pair of gaudy golden scissors. After the dog and pony show, Tex could hardly believe his eyes; people came from all over the state to experience the art, music, food and coffee and become a part of the story. Several different news outlets attended to interview different artists and customers. One news channel conducted an interview with Jimmy inside of Toucans. Tex walked down to my coffee shop where I was hard at work making cappuccinos for a young couple with an expensive baby stroller. All the seats on the newly constructed farmers porch were filled with people enjoying coffee and pastry. Tex was so proud of me, all he could muster to say was,

"Can you believe this kid?"

"No sir, no sir, I can't," I replied, as I handed Tex a coffee on the house. Of course Tex wouldn't accept a free cup so he left a five-dollar gratuity on the counter, and threatened me with bodily harm or even eviction, if I so much as attempted to give it back.

"Thanks old man."

"No, thank you, kid" he said, gazing out the window to people watch. Raising his cup in a nod of appreciation, he walked out to relish the momentous occasion.

The opening weekend far exceeded everyone's wildest expectations. The artists were all very pleased with how much they sold. Jimmy was delighted with the number of customers that visited. Not only did people go there for the freshest oysters in town, but for Jimmy's fisherman charm and his uncanny ability to weave a tale about his exploits on the water. He told Tex that he hadn't shucked that many oysters in years.

"My hands are killing me."

"From shucking oysters or counting your money?" Tex quipped

"Hopefully the latter, soon," Jimmy replied with a smile.

One of the unexpected highlights of the weekend occurred when a few different aspiring musicians showed up and asked

Tex if they could perform near the group of picnic tables. Of course he obliged their request, and showed them where they could perform. The older of the three teens, a black kid, asked Tex politely if they could ask for tips.

"Why else would you be here kid? Of course you can."
"Thanks mister."
"You're welcome son, and the name is Tex. Now play me some music."

The three teenagers erected a drum set made from discarded buckets and milk crate seats. Just then, as life would have it, another teenager strolled up and unbuckled his large case and removed a guitar. He placed the empty guitar case in front of him leaving it open for people to show their appreciation, after asking Tex if it was all right to play. Again, the answer was yes. After a few hours of playing on opposite sides of the courtyard, one of the drummers invited the guitarist over to play with them. Soon after, they were playing together as if they had rehearsed together for years. Tex was the first person to throw a five-dollar bill into the guitar case turned tip jar for the newly formed group.

The next day a beautiful Cuban girl showed up by herself with a hula-hoop, a pocket full of hope and asked Tex the same question. He answered in the same fashion, but referred to her as honey. She tugged on his heartstrings by informing him that she had run away from an abusive boyfriend in Key West. She had left with a broken heart, a broken nose, a hula hoop and a determination never to be treated like that again by another man. When Tex asked her how she ended up in Rhode Island, she replied,

"Well, my aunt lives here and told me that I was always welcome. I guess she felt compelled to help me, or maybe it was pity because her sister abandoned me and forced me to grow up in group homes when I was a kid."

"Sorry honey. Well, you have a home here too. I'm starting to think that we are all misfits; you'll fit in just fine."

"I'm Tex, and you are?"
"Rhythm."
"What?"
She repeated, "My name is Rhythm; I told you my mother was messed up," causing them both to laugh.

"Thanks again Mister, I needed this."
"Tex, call me Tex, none of this mister shit."
"Ok Tex, well, thanks again. Do I owe you rent, or how does this work?""Don't worry about that. Get on your feet first."
"I can't thank you enough Tex, You're an angel; you just saved my life."

Tex just smiled at the universe and walked away while telling her we are all angels.
Most performers honor an unwritten rule of keeping distance between each other, so as not to impose or affect each others' tips, but Local Motion had a different vibe. The boy with

the guitar came over and asked Rhythm to join them. She walked over, not knowing what to expect. "Can you dance to the rhythm of a song?" the singer asked.

"If you only knew!" she replied confidently. "Can you sing to the beat of my hips?"

"Oh, it's on!" he said, as they accepted each other's challenge. With that, they began to perform as if was meant to be. Her cinnamon colored hips that appeared to have been kissed by Apollo himself, flowed like waves on the ocean to the singer's soulful voice, and the sounds of the guitar and drums. She moved as if to defy the existence of the very bones that were designed to restrict such movements.

After a few weeks of selling coffee under my belt, the business continued to expand. Not only did the artists and customers visit for great tasting coffee, but my establishment became a popular stop for regulars on their way to their cubicle for eight and a half hours. People were becoming aware of the power they possessed as consumers. No longer were they patronizing a coffee conglomerate with over twenty thousand locations. No, they came to my shop by virtue of receiving a great product and supporting someone local. I decided to cut back my hours at the office even more, and opened the coffee shop on Wednesdays and Thursdays as well.

"If this keeps up, I'll resign by the fourth of July." I promised Mary.

"You can either follow your dream, or work for someone who followed theirs," she concurred.

Tex and I still met for our ritual morning coffee. The only difference now was that Mary was included. The conversations revolved mostly around Local Motion and the inner workings of the community. Gone were the days of me bitching to Tex about how unfair life had been or how my ex was treating me that week. She was nothing more than a distant memory, fading with each passing day. Once I made the mistake of telling Tex about how lucky I was, to which Tex quoted Samuel Goldwyn by saying "The harder I work, the luckier I get."

One morning while Mary and I were sitting at Chico's table, Tex knocked on the door holding a perfectly folded flag. I hoisted my bodies dead weight and prepared the coffee, I began to reminisce how I'd thought it was the worst day of my life, when I had pulled into the dirt driveway of the cabins, only to realize that it was the most important U-turn of my life.

"I'll never forget how I felt walking though my house, knowing it would be the last time I heard the hardwood floor crack in the same place where it had always made noise. I remember looking at my children's toothbrushes in their holders, I actually picked them up and gently kissed them. I kissed a friggin' toothbrush, Tex. I left with one picture of my kids, the picture from the beach, a coffee maker, a box of worn out clothes and a record player. Fifteen years of a partnership fit into my backseat. Now as I look back, it was all supposed to happen exactly the way it did. I have no clue what made me take that picture on the beach that day, or make the U-turn into this place, but something told me to do so. I hated this place. It was an eyesore that I drove by every day of my marriage. We made fun every time we saw a car here. Now my car has been here for a year, and I couldn't be more proud. This place was the epitome of failure, but I still pulled in despite how I felt. Now as I look back, this was all supposed to be. This was my boulevard. This is my story. I couldn't have written or lived it without you two."

"I love you kid," Tex humbly responded.
"I think we all were brought together to save one another," Mary said as she dunked her Stella Doro in the coffee.

"It's just so crazy to think that if I kept driving and moved into a third floor apartment none of this would have occurred."

"The universe wouldn't have allowed that to happen," Mary assured.
"God has a plan for all of us Hemingway, that includes you," Tex added. Just then it dawned on me that's precisely what the court officer had said before I started this journey.
"I guess this was our destiny. I'm just glad we listened to the universe and its omens; at times I couldn't see the ocean through the water, but with your help I got though it" I replied.

"Hope dies last kid, remember?"

"Sure do Tex, sure do."

"I'm not afraid anymore. I've accepted that there is a greater power in charge leading each of us in the proper direction. How else could someone explain this?"

"That's great James, I'm so proud of you and all that you have accomplished.

"Thanks Mary, Honestly, thank you.

"We all have a compass; some people just follow theirs. Others are much too smart," Mary said.

"I would love to stay here and listen to you two lovebirds, but this flag won't raise itself." Tex said.

As moved as I was with the depth of the conversation and the sight of an old war veteran walking across a yard with a flag intended to be raised, I walked over to my stack of records and flipped through until I found the only bagpipe album in my collection. I placed it on the turntable and rotated the volume knob until it stopped. As Tex began to clip the flag onto the pole, the sounds of Amazing Grace filled the morning air. Tex continued to raise old glory with pride. As the flag came to a rest at the top, a gust of wind snapped the red, white, and blue canvas to attention. Tex turned around to see me with my arm around Mary standing on the porch. Tex raised his right arm and presented a salute with robotic precision. I returned my best, but much-practice-needed salute, and then went on with the day.

I kept my promise to Mary and resigned from my hamster wheel job. I was sick of being an insignificant spoke on the wheel of my company. Now, I was the hub where all spokes began and ended. I had planned to stay closed on Mondays, but Mary convinced me to reconsider, reminding me that most people hate their jobs and are most typically unhappy that the weekend is over and the workweek just beginning. Most dread that they have five days to go.

"These people need you on Mondays James."
I laughed and completely agreed.

I decided instead to close on Tuesdays, both to recharge my batteries, but also to spend some much treasured time with Mary and my daughters. Most Monday nights we would stay at Mary's and enjoy a nice breakfast in the morning. I would rise first and prepare egg whites with spinach; we always split the English muffin. I made breakfast, not because Mary chose not to, but because I saw this as my only creative outlet. I couldn't draw a straight line, let alone a picture. Mary patiently tried to teach me using several different mediums, but soon realized that it was best just to allow me to make the coffee and eggs. She always set the table by creating sculptures with napkins that never failed to impressed, and after each meal she would contribute by clearing the dishes, but we always washed them by hand, together as a team.

Our relationship was pure and genuine. It didn't revolve around money or inanimate objects to inflate either one's fragile ego. Both made each other feel worthy of their love;

we finally experienced trust as strong as heated lead on metal, insecurities and phone checking were an immature aspect of time since past that we would never revisit. This was a relationship between people that cared even more for each other than for themselves.

"Do you want to get married Mary?" I asked while sitting across from her. This wasn't a question of engagement on bended knee, but simply a question out of curiosity.

"Not a chance," Mary answered as quickly as a gunslinger could draw his weapon in the Wild West.

"Oh good, neither do I," I replied smiling.
We both just sat at Mary's table looking each other with the satisfaction of knowing that both of us had found our best friend.

"Honey, can you please hand me the hot sauce?"
"Of course I can, my love."

Often times, the universe bestows a kiss upon each of us.

It is our purpose in life, as the beneficiary, to acknowledge such reverence.

One must always remember to keep one's soul, and the soul of the universe, intertwined.

Furthermore, remember that there are no coincidences in our short lives, just reminders that there is a higher energy guiding us. It informs us of its presence by creating a boulevard for our lives and allowing us to discover our story.

Be open . . Be aware . . Be thankful.

Jason Felix DeCesare

By Haleigh

Stars.

My six year old daughter sat with me on countless every other weekends while I toiled away at this novel. One morning she asked if she could write her own. I think she earned the opportunity.....

People do many stuff like getting necklaces, they buy stuff in stores. They buy stores.

Apples are healthy for humans.

People like other things, but sometimes they aren't the same.

People sleep in beds.

Friends are always together.

You paint houses whatever color you want, like light green.

Fruit are healthy for all people.

Sharks eat people.

Colors are everywhere.

Some cats like to swim.

Love is love.

Made in the USA
Middletown, DE
20 May 2016